Who hasn't thought Pride and Prejudice could use more dragons?

D1320071

The Dragons of Kellynch

Maria Grace

White Soup Press

Published by: White Soup Press

The Dragons of Kellynch
Copyright © 2020 Maria Grace

For information, address
author.MariaGrace@gmail.com

ISBN-13: **978-0-9997984-2-3** (White Soup Press)

Author's Website: RandomBitsofFaascination.com
Email address: Author.MariaGrace@gmail.com

Dedication

For my husband and sons.
You have always believed in me.

1
Chapter

May 1809

THE SOUNDS OF animated conversation filtered into the corridor as Anne slowly approached the morning room. One did not rush about, even if she were quite hungry, or so Father insisted. Pleasing and graceful movements and a columnar posture were always necessary and appropriate. Morning light poured through the doorways, painting the navy and burgundy hall carpeting and the edge of her white muslin skirts in pale gold. Tempting aromas wafted through the door: fresh buns and jam, tea and coffee, and perhaps, yes, a plate of cold ham. Her stomach rumbled.

She peeked in. Warm sunshine filled the room exactly as Mama had anticipated when she had the room papered in sky-blue paper hangings with small birds and clouds. She had loved the notion of bringing a bit of the garden inside whenever she could.

Father occupied his usual seat at the table, near the door, scanning the newspaper, probably the society pages, his favorite and perhaps only reading material—aside from the *Baronetage,* of course. Mary, in a plain, rumpled morning dress, and Elizabeth, in a fine half-dress gown, ready to received callers, sat on opposite sides of the small, round, dark oak table, too far from the window for the light to be agreeable for needlework. They both hated sewing.

Elizabeth stared at the wall over Mary's head, ignoring the journal and several sheets of foolscap on the table before her. Elizabeth's latest watercolor, which Father had lately framed, hung between Mama's landscapes on the sky-blue wall. Elizabeth's work was nothing to Mama's, but that was not the sort of thing one mentioned.

"How well it looks, now it is properly hung—do you not agree, Anne?" Elizabeth arched her eyebrow and directed her gaze to the empty chair near the window. The one she expected Anne to hurry and occupy.

"I am glad you are so pleased with it," Anne muttered as she sidled between Mary and the sideboard, pausing to serve herself toast and tea on Mama's breakfast china—ivory with a band of vine roses around the edges.

Elizabeth glowered, never one to appreciate a neglected compliment, while Mary's raised eyebrows and pursed lips probably suppressed a snicker. She often complained that Elizabeth was too used to compliments.

Anne sat down and dabbed a bit of blackberry jam on her toast.

"I have been meaning to talk to you Anne." Elizabeth sat up very straight and pulled back her shoulders. Lovely, she was trying to look like Mama, a bad sign indeed. "About dinner last night."

"Surely you are not going to find fault with the Musgroves? Perhaps it was a little unseemly for Mrs. Musgrove to go on about their concerns for Dick—"

"I am not concerned for Mrs. Musgrove's behavior. That is her husband's problem. I am referring to yours." Elizabeth slapped the edge of the table.

Mary stared at her plate, her lips pressed hard, no doubt trying to hide traces of amusement.

"All I did was listen to her."

"And that is the problem. What right, what expectation does that woman have to bend your ear with such talk? Truly, it is unseemly in the best of lights and far worse if one gives it any consideration."

Anne blinked and sipped her tea—a mite bitter this morning. "What is unseemly about having a modicum of compassion on the poor woman's nerves? They are our friends."

"Our friends, but not our rank. Our rank, Anne! Remember that." Elizabeth glanced at Father.

"To what end shall I remember it?" That was probably not the right remark to offer if she wanted the conversation to end.

"Let her find an old aunt or cousin to whine and whinge upon, not one of a station above her own. I should not have to tell you this. I will not have you being an embarrassment to us when we are invited out. Father agrees."

Father peeked above his newspaper and grunted.

"You see." Elizabeth looked down her sharp nose as she rifled through the papers before her. "Here, I have a list of things I need for you to do today." She handed Anne a carefully penned list. Perfect penmanship was another of Elizabeth's many accomplishments.

"Calls to the tenants?" Anne traced down the list with her finger. "Visits to the shops?"

"They need to be done, and you are the proper person to do it."

"But these are tasks for the mistress of the house."

"I have other things to do today." Elizabeth was ever so forceful about insisting that assuming Mama's role was her privilege and duty. Clearly, she preferred the privilege to the duty.

"What is more important than acting in your role?"

Mary sniffed, not looking up from her plate. "She expects the modiste to come around and fit her new gown."

"Here? Why would she come here? The cost—"

Elizabeth snorted and tossed her head. "Why should I be bothered about that? It is customary for her to come to me. I do not wish to be seen—"

"You were happy enough to go to her shop to order the gown."

"That is enough, Anne." Elizabeth spoke her name as a reprimand. "Truly it is. I do not know why you are so disagreeable today. Just do as I have asked."

"But I have things to do as well."

"What have you to do?"

Anne braced her elbow on the table and her forehead in her hand. Did she really want to defend the calls she intended to make to Elizabeth and likely Father as well? Even if she did, what were the chances that she might actually win the argument? She swallowed back her sigh. "I will make the calls."

"Be sure and check with Mrs. Trent. She and Cook are packing a basket for you to take whilst paying those calls. It would not do to pay a call from the manor empty-handed."

"I imagine you have already given orders for the carriage to be readied for me?" Anne closed her eyes and took a long sip of bitter tea.

"You want the carriage? You are so fond of a good walk." There was that down-her-nose look again.

Anne stood. It would be satisfying to leave without further remark, but that would probably spark even more conversation. "I will see to it myself."

She held her breath as she made her way to the door. If she were quiet enough, perhaps there would be no more conversation.

"Oh, Anne!" Mary waved at her. "When you return, I need your help mending a gown. You know how clumsy I am with a needle."

That meant she wanted Anne to do it for her.

Anne ducked her head and scurried out.

Three, no, it was four hours later, Anne stood in the doorway of Kellynch's oldest cottage. It was a quaint little wattle and daub, thatched roof structure, two stories tall, but they were very short stories— Anne's head nearly brushed the ceiling in the claustrophobic main room. Clean and tidy within but hardly well-appointed.

Whilst the tenant—a widow with three young children—did not complain, the roof and front door clearly needed repair. It was right to expect these structures would keep wind and rain out. Perhaps a visit to Mr. Shepherd, who often managed such affairs for Father, would be in order.

Tomorrow.

No more calls today. No more forced conversations. No more offering gifts from the kitchen that were less than Anne would have wanted to give. What was more mortifying: the tenants' gratitude or her embarrassment at Elizabeth's meagre offerings? What did it matter? Mortification was exhausting, and she needed air.

She dismissed the driver and carriage, watching it trundle away down the narrow lane—if Elizabeth found out, she would hear about it for weeks—but she needed to walk, and walk she would.

A late spring breeze—cool and refreshing with hints of green scents—caressed her face, welcoming her onto the slim road. Dust rose up at each footstep, painting the white hem of her skirt gray; it was barely noticeable in the dappled sun that slipped between the arching hardwood branches overhead, clothed with new green leaves. She drew in a large breath of fresh air, bracing and restoring. Much better.

No more succumbing to the bidding of others. She would be in command of her life, at least for the next few minutes.

"Good afternoon, Miss Anne."

Or not.

She jumped and turned toward the voice. "Oh, Mr. Musgrove, it is you! I did not hear you approaching."

"Pray forgive me for startling you." He bowed from his shoulders, a round-faced, ruddy young man, with chubby cheeks that made him appear more boyish than the heir to Uppercross, the second most consequential property of the county, should have appeared. His blowsy, tousled hair, in some sort of a haircut with owl in its name that stuck out wildly beneath his hat only added to the effect, making him difficult to take seriously at times.

"I suppose I was lost in thought. Father has often warned me to pay better attention whilst I am out."

"I am going to the village. Might you be going in a similar direction?" He gestured toward the road ahead.

"Indeed, Elizabeth has several errands for me."

He rolled his eyes just a mite, just enough to suggest he understood without her saying anything more. "Might I walk with you then?"

Saying no would have been impolite, but it was tempting nonetheless. "Of course."

For several minutes, they walked along in silent step with one another, gravel and leaves crunching underfoot.

"My mother wondered if Sir Walter found the roast pork to his liking last night." Charles clasped his hands behind his back.

Dry, stringy and flavorless were definitely not to Father's liking. "It was a most memorable meal, he told me. He was particularly fond of the sauce served with the roast."

"Mama noticed he had quite a bit of it. Would you find it amusing to know that she wrote herself a note to make sure that it is available the next time Sir Walter joins us for dinner?" He flashed his brows in a knowing sort of way.

"That is very good of her. Your mother is an excellent hostess." It was true—it was hardly her fault that her cook ruined the roast.

"May I tell her you said that? It would please her very much."

"I would not suspend any pleasure of hers."

Charles laughed softly. "Of course, you would not. You are all that is good and kind."

"Do not resort to flattery. It does not become you." She kicked a small clump of dirt. It bounced and danced until it came to rest on a patch of grass beside the lane. The sweet scent of hawthorn bushes wafted on the breeze. They were approaching Lady Russell's garden.

"It is not idle flattery, certainly not. You ought to know I am not given to such things. No, you should have heard what my mother said about you after you left last night."

Anne gulped. One rarely wanted to know what was said about oneself.

"She and my sisters both went on and on about how gracious you were to listen to Mother waffle on about Dick's latest misadventure."

Misadventure really was an understatement, a very kind, gentle one, much like Charles' nature in general, but still an understatement. Mischief at school that involved the local constabulary was a very serious thing indeed. But it was hardly surprising. Dick was hardly disciplined enough for a student's life.

"Mother, and Father as well, are at sixes and sevens with my brother, you know. They have heard so much criticism of him that it was ever so pleasing that you could just listen without rebuke or remark. Thank you for that."

Anne blushed. What would Charles think to have heard Elizabeth this morning?

"Anne, is that you?" Lady Russell bustled toward

them. Tall and slender, in blue muslin and a hat with bobbing feathers that almost bounced against her face, she curtsied as she stopped beside them. "Good day, Mr. Musgrove."

"Good day, Lady Russell." He peered at her intently as he bowed, an odd expression on his face.

"Why ever do you look at me as though you do not know me? I am the same woman you know quite well and see regularly in the neighborhood." Lady Russell spoke softly, deliberately, looking directly into his eyes. She was a handsome woman with large bright eyes and pleasant regular features, who barely owned her age—traits which Father greatly approved.

"Yes, of course. Pray do forgive me. I was just not expecting to see you." Charles eased back half a step.

"I do not understand why not when you are walking past my own garden." She wrinkled her nose, a mite larger and longer than it ideally should have been. All agreed it was her least attractive feature. "Might I trouble you to come inside for a few moments, Anne? I have mislaid my glasses and have something I need you to read to me."

What joy, another requirement.

Anne glanced at Charles, who tipped his hat. "I have monopolized your company long enough. I will not keep you from your friend. Good day." He sauntered away.

Lady Russell tucked her arm in Anne's as they turned toward Kellynch Cottage, the largest and best-appointed tenant property on Kellynch. Far more than a typical two-up two-down, four room affair, it boasted several bedrooms, a morning room and dining room, as well as a parlor and drawing room, rivaling the dower house in its improvements. Lady

Russell and her late husband, Sir Henry, who had occupied that cottage for as long as Anne could remember would have settled for no less. But it was good to see Mama's great friend comfortable in her widowhood.

"I confess, I am a little surprised to see you walking with Charles Musgrove." Lady Russell clucked her tongue in the way she often did when perplexed.

Anne struggled to keep up with Lady Russell's very long steps along the stony garden path. "I had been calling upon tenants, and we were both walking to the village."

"If he were any more clever, I would say that it was contrived on his part."

"How can you say such a thing about him? The Musgroves are totally artless."

"You think that a compliment?" Lady Russell snorted—rather unladylike of her really.

"In this case, yes I do. I thought you liked the Uppercross family. Why do you seem so displeased today?"

"I am not displeased, truly I am not, only a bit startled. I had thought it might take a little longer to happen, that is all."

"For what to happen?" Anne stopped and pulled her arm away from Lady Russell. She drew in a deep breath of hawthorn-perfumed air. Perhaps the sweet scent would also sweeten her temper.

"The boy likes you; can you not see that?"

"Our families have been friends for a very long time."

"Do not be a ninny! You know what I mean. It is time for him to settle down. You are pretty enough, well-connected, and convenient. What more could he ask for?"

Convenient? "That hardly sounds like a compliment." Certainly, Wentworth had never thought her merely convenient. He had actually had feelings for her.

A familiar ache opened near her heart and wound its way through her chest. She gritted her teeth. Definitely not a subject to discuss with Lady Russell.

"I meant no offense my dear, you should know that of me. I am only interested in what is best for you."

"So, I imagine you wish to warn me away from him." Anne stopped and locked her gaze with Lady Russell who waited for Anne to back down.

She did not.

Finally, Lady Russell blinked. "By no means. Why would I do such a thing? In order to secure her future, a young woman must marry well. If anything, I am pleased. He is a good enough sort of fellow and would—"

Anne lifted her open hands. "Stop. Pray just stop. I do not wish to have this conversation with you, not now and perhaps not ever."

"You are still angry with me …"

"I have no wish to discuss that either. Pray excuse me. You will have to find someone else to read your letter to you. I must go." Anne dropped a tiny curtsy and dashed through the garden to the dirt road, not slowing until Kellynch Cottage was out of sight.

Lady Russell would never admit to her error over Wentworth.

At the time, her arguments seemed sound: a sailor of no fortune was far too big a risk for Anne to place her future—and that of her children—upon. The years had proven Lady Russell wrong, though. Anne had been a fool to listen, and no amount of time, or attentions from a man like Charles Musgrove, would ever change that.

Chapter 2

Gibraltar, May 1809

WENTWORTH PAUSED TO adjust the canvas bag slung over his shoulder. The torches within made it an annoying, awkward bundle, bouncing along his back. A crisp breeze, smelling of salt air, forced its way through the trees, rustling branches and leaves as if to remind him that he should take care; he was merely a visitor to Gibraltar.

Being landside never felt quite right, not since those heady days spent near Kellynch when he was tempted to tie himself to the shore once more. That would not happen again. The sea was home to him now, and, if he had his way, would be for the rest of his life.

He dragged his sleeve across his forehead, leaving a dark stain across the drab fabric. Hot, but not bloody hot. Just past its zenith, the sun's kiss left him sweating and decidedly inelegant. But what did that matter out here on the side of an island mountain? There was little elegant company to be found. Some who pretended to sophistication to be sure, but little of the real stuff.

It was not as though he had any want for stylish company, though. Sampling it once was quite enough. Miss Anne Elliot had left him with sufficient heart-ache for a lifetime.

Inconstant, weak-willed, mild-mannered, spine-less…

No, giving into those thoughts would do him no good now nor probably ever. He pinched his temples. Enough hours, days, weeks had been lost in those resentments. It was high time to leave those behind. Just as he had left England behind.

Damn, there were days he still managed to miss them both.

He tamped his walking stick down hard on the rocky path and continued his trudge up the steep trail. Another salty breeze rattled the surrounding pine and olive trees, carrying some of the heat away from the back of his neck. Quiet, the woods were so very quiet. How long had it been since he had been genuinely alone?

Months, easily months. There was no solitude aboard ship.

The *Laconia* was safely tucked away in the port, en-joying some needed repairs as his men partook in leave. The opportunity to be away should have been restorative, a welcome bit of relaxation from the pres-sures of a ship captain's duties.

It should have been. But it left him far too much

opportunity to think, to be alone with his thoughts and worse, his feelings. He shook away the twitchy feeling in his shoulders. Everyone was better off when that could be avoided, especially himself. No, he needed something to do, some occupation to capture his attention away from those thoughts, one that required his full attention.

Where better to do that than St. Michael's cave? Exploring it with only the light of his torch, fighting the obstacles alone; one mistake, one fall, one doused torch from death in the chill, dank, darkness. A proper and welcome distraction for certain.

Such an amazing, glorious place it was—how could he not wish to revisit it? In the flicker of the torch light, astounding, unearthly structures towered all around him, glistening water droplets like gems twinkling, beckoning him in farther. Perhaps one day he would attempt to explore further into the caverns—but there were already rumors of men lost forever in the bottomless recesses. His heart might have been ill-used, but not so much as to occasion losing himself in the darkness.

At least not on most days.

He was getting close. The scent of damp limestone rode the edge of the wind now, replacing the saltiness. Cool and earthy, it had an appeal all its own, rather like the cave itself. He shaded his eyes and peered down the trail, the craggy, overhung cave entrance just visible.

A piercing scream, like a cat whose tail had been stepped on, ricocheted against the rocks, echoing and amplifying before it faded into the stony landscape. The raucous chittering of the local apes followed.

Blast and bloody botheration!

A screaming cat he could have ignored, no matter how fond he was of the creatures, but not those frightful Barbary apes. Irrational though it was, those dreadful beasts with their mocking laughs and their not-quite-human faces—he shuddered and quickened his step. Nothing should be left to the mercies of those little monsters.

The cave's mouth rose up before him and, just beside it, a mob of the stinking, tawny-furred little apes converged around something, shrieking and poking at it. Another feline scream pierced the air from the midst of them.

Wentworth brandished his walking stick, swinging it into the middle of the pack. Several satisfying thuds and yelps followed. "Get away! Out, out the lot of you! Be gone with you!"

The apes, cowards that they were, screamed and feinted, but finally ran from him and his stick.

"Good riddance! Now stay away!" He shook his stick in the air.

An ape laughed from the branches above.

He stomped toward the trees. If that foul creature—

"Mrooooo." A spine-chilling, plaintive cry, pain mixed with fear.

He turned toward the rock face. Leathery egg shards lay scattered on the rocky ground. In the center, huddled against the rocks, a slimy black ball of fur, the size of a small cat.

"Mrrow! Mrrrow!"

Prickles rose on the back of his neck. It could not be, could it?

Wentworth crossed the distance in three brisk strides, chest aching. "Poor thing—weren't you beat all hollow? That won't fadge at all!" He knelt beside the creature.

"Meeerow!" Great gold eyes stared up at him as the creature hissed.

"I know you've had an awful row there, but you have nothing more to fear, little fellow. Those apes are gone." He extended his left hand, fingers curled toward himself.

It reached out to sniff his fingers, long and deep, then his hand and wrist. A long, forked tongue licked his fingertips.

"What an excellent little fellow." He nudged it toward his hand, his heart beating so hard the creature must surely be able to hear it.

"Mrrow!" It crawled, gooey and cold, into his palm and wrapped its long, black, serpentine tail around his wrist. Tiny claws on its front paws grabbed his shirt sleeve for purchase. He lifted the creature to look eye-to-eye with him.

Its front half, though matted and wet with egg slime, appeared to be a large black kitten with huge glittering eyes and a very pathetic expression. Extra-large front paws bore noticeable thumb toes. The rear half, covered in glistening ebony scales, should have been paired with a huge black snake. But it was firmly attached to the front half of a newly-hatched tatzelwurm.

Wentworth's hand trembled just a bit, and his breath caught in his throat.

The little dragon pushed its cold, soppy head into his face and rubbed it along Wentworth's stubbled cheek. "Hungry!"

Of course! How could he have not thought! With his right hand, he reached into his bag. Just a little farther—yes! Wrapping paper crinkled under his fingers. He pulled a small parcel from his bag. Thank goodness he had planned ahead—granted, not for a dragon hatching, but food was food.

The tatzelwurm began rumbling. Purring, and he had not yet been fed? What a splendid little creature!

He wrestled the parcel open one-handed and pulled off a piece of ham. Not the ideal first meal for a newly-hatched dragon, but it was all he had. He held up the tidbit.

The creature squeaked happily and gobbled the morsel down so fast it almost caught Wentworth's fingertip in his teeth. Hatching hunger should not be underestimated.

Who would have thought Croft's training him to befriend a companion dragon would prove useful after so many years—and rejections—and in such a place as this?

"Mooore?" The tip of its tail flicked against Wentworth's arm.

"Of course." Wentworth offered another bite. And another and another, until the little creature's belly was quite distended, and its eyes blinked lazily.

"Mrooo." The tatzelwurm yawned, breath smelling like ham. How could a creature so small have such a very large mouth?

"Now I should think it is time to clean you up. Would that be acceptable?" When no protest registered, he fished a handkerchief from his pocket and scrubbed egg slime from the rich black fur until a big-eyed, long fanged, ball of black fluff stood in his hand. "What a handsome little fellow you are."

It licked its shoulder, then stretched its neck for a scratch under the chin.

Wentworth obliged. "Do you know how you came to be here? Did you hatch in a nest?"

"Just broke shell. Awful *things* dropped me here." Its voice was surprisingly deep and just a mite hoarse.

"I see." Wentworth scratched behind the tufted, furry ears. "I am sorry, that is a bloody difficult way to make a start."

It—he, the creature was male—rubbed his cheek, against Wentworth's petting hand, rearing back slightly on his muscular tail to reach, purring so loudly, Wentworth's chest rumbled in time.

"What would you like to do now?" Wentworth held his breath. Let not this not be as the last time.

He blinked up at Wentworth. "No like *things*."

"I hate them."

"You keep *things* away?"

"Most of the time I live on a ship where there are no *things*." Wentworth sat back against the rock of the hillside, drawing the tatzelwurm close.

"No *things?* Like that." He purred and licked Wentworth's palm with a rough, forked tongue. "What ship?"

How did one explain a ship to a newborn dragon? "Like a nest that floats on the water. I go many places."

The wyrmling cocked his head to and fro. "To places with *things?*"

Wentworth shuddered. "No. This is the only place I have ever been with *things*."

"Go with you?" The little chirrup at the end of his question sounded so hopeful. He nestled in closer to Wentworth's chest.

"Ship's cats are very welcome. Black ones are considered particularly lucky and ones with many toes like you are especially welcome." He stroked the top of the tatzelwurm's head. "I should think you would be well-liked there. You would of course have to tell my shipmates you are a large cat."

"Can do." A cool serpentine tail slipped under the edge of Wentworth's coat and fluffy paws folded against his chest.

"What do you think of the name Laconia? It is the name of my ship. Landed dragons share the name of their estate. It seems a ship's dragon should share the name of the ship."

"Yes. Good." Laconia purred and rested his chin on his paws. "Sleep now. Stay you." A moment later, he drew in the deep breaths of sleep.

Wentworth cradled Laconia to his chest and stared up into the clear sky, eyes prickling. Had this really all just happened? He draped his arm over Laconia who rumbled just a little louder.

There was a baby dragon asleep in his arms. A dragon—one that called him Friend! And he only had to beat off a pack of apes for the privilege. He dragged his free arm across his eyes. He was a true Dragon Mate now, just like Croft and Sophy always insisted he would be. Who would have thought?

Laconia snored softly, in time with his breathing, and half-opened one eye to stare adoringly at Wentworth.

How long had he envied the Crofts for their Dragon Friend, White? Not that he would ever have admitted it aloud, but he had been jealous. It was hard to hear dragons, to be a member of the Blue Order, and not have a dragon Friend.

No more though, not with this fine fellow as his companion. He stroked Laconia's silky fur, right behind his ears; Laconia closed his eye again and purred in his sleep.

His crew would welcome the little creature—truly a sign of good fortune for their next voyage—especially when he told them he had rescued it from the hands of those horrid apes. Most of his men detested the creatures as much as he did. Though they had been enjoying good fortune, a lucky "cat" to reinforce that sense would not hurt. The men always performed better when they thought luck was in their favor.

Wentworth chuckled. No doubt they would spoil the little creature when his back was turned. Laconia would like that. What dragon would object—especially after making such a start in the world?

He leaned his head back and closed his eyes, warmth—was that contentment?—surging over him in waves, carried on Laconia's purrs. Dragon thunder! Years, it had been years since he had felt this way—or any way at all.

It was good to feel warm and alive again.

3 Chapter

June, 1809

IN THE MONTH that followed, the Elliots and the Musgroves dined together three more times: once at Kellynch, once at Uppercross and once at Barnfield, a place barely large enough to be considered an estate according to Father. Four morning calls were made between the ladies of Kellynch and Uppercross, with Elizabeth and Mary included on two of them. Several card parties and assorted encounters in the village made a total of at least a dozen meetings between the two estates. A great deal of society between two houses otherwise unconnected to one another. Every time it came up in conversation with Lady Russell, she cocked her head with a knowing look and clucked her tongue.

At least that was the limit of her meddling. A

blessing to be sure.

The warm summer breeze carried the scent—and perhaps, if it were possible—the taste of the blooming peonies that Lady Elliot had planted in the broad flowerbed on the east side of the garden to celebrate the birth of each of her daughters. Did Father know that was why she planted them? Probably not.

Bees darted from blossom to blossom, filling the garden with a low hum. Anne's white muslin skirts caught on the abundant green leaves as she picked her way through the sunshine and blossoms, the path she trod barely discernable between the spreading bushes.

Mama had placed many such footpaths through her garden, as though to tempt or perhaps test her visitors. Mama always had a fondness for those souls curious and adventurous.

People very unlike her middle daughter.

Once, when Anne had been very small, she had encountered Mama and Lady Russell talking to the colorful little birds that darted through the garden, acting as though they were having a conversation with them, as though the birds were talking back. Mama even went so far as to call them her little garden dragons!

But when Anne dashed in to join them, asking to see the dragons too, Lady Russell had given her such a very queer look. Even the birds twittered at her strangely.

Lady Russell crouched in front of Anne, looking directly into her eyes. "You have such a vivid imagination, dear. But there are no dragons here. There is no such creature; you must not say such outlandish things." Mama had agreed.

Apparently, she was not interesting enough to be

included in their little game.

Anne buried her face in a large pink peony blossom. The soft petals tickled her nose as she sighed. Would Mama approve of her now—or would she have found Anne as dull and boring as Elizabeth and Father did? She lifted her head toward the sunshine, eyes closed, and drew a deep breath of intoxicating garden air.

Miss Hamilton—no it was Mrs. Smith now—had always loved peonies. In her most recent letter, she mentioned planting them in the mews behind the townhouse she and her husband shared in Bath. What would it be like to be married and manage a home of her own, planting what she wanted, where she wanted it? Heady stuff, indeed.

"Miss Anne?" What was he doing in the garden?

Charles Musgrove had been appearing at Kellynch with some regularity, calling weekly it seemed. Whether that was a good thing or not, remained to be determined.

"Miss Anne?" He stopped, a little breathless, in front of her, sweat trickling down the side of his round face. His cheeks were a mite redder than usual and the starch on his cravat a bit wilted, probably from the heat of the day. Father would not approve of his color nor his starch.

"Good day, Mr. Musgrove." She dipped in a small curtsied and inclined her head.

"It is a good day. Quite a good day, I think. Would you care for a walk in the garden?" He gestured back toward the main path, his deep green coat blending in with the leaves and stems.

"Why thank you, I should like that." It was a bit of a lie, on several counts. Was it wrong to be disappointed he wanted to leave her mother's covert path?

That Charles would prefer the more well-traveled ways was not surprising nor even wrong in the most basic sense of the word. But it was a bit dreary—was that the right way to describe it? Perhaps that was not fair. He was a dependable, regular sort of man. Upright and sensible. Kind and responsible. Predictable and dull. Nothing like—

She hid a clenched fist in her skirts. No! No, those thoughts offered no comfort nor did they change the past. Nothing would change that; nothing could undo what had been done. Lady Russell's counsel had come from the most sympathetic and affectionate place it could have, however great her error. Dwelling upon it only produced discontent, something that could easily breed bitterness and lead her in a dangerous direction.

No one wanted the company of a bitter old-maid.

No, she was not an old-maid, not yet. But a girl headed for the shelf could not entertain even the hint of bitterness, lest it seal her fate.

"Do you prefer to return to the house?" He stopped and gazed upon her quite intently; at least it was intently for him. Nothing like the intense gazes Wentworth had offered her …

"No, not at all. Why do you ask?"

"You have a most peculiar expression right now, rather as though you are a bit uncomfortable or discomposed."

"Forgive me. Being in my mother's garden sometimes makes me think of her and of the past which, at times, can lead to a touch of melancholy." Though not complete, the answer was true enough for the moment.

He nodded and resumed a slow walk. "I understand. My mother is apt to a similar sensation when she considers my brother, Dick. I am afraid it seems that school has not settled well with him."

"The new establishment your father chose for him has not worked out?"

"Father is reluctant to say as much. Dick's notes say very little and are few and far between, as they say. But the headmaster dispatched a letter recently and, judging by Father's mood after reading it, I cannot imagine that the news was good."

"I am sorry to hear that. I understood that your sisters enjoy being away at school very much and were even looking forward to the next term. I look upon my years at school with such fondness; it is difficult to conceive of someone who would not."

"True enough, but I understand that a girls' school is a far more genteel sort of establishment than a boys'. The rigors of Greek and Latin, you know, can be very taxing."

What he meant to say was that his brother did not appear to have the capacity to learn such elevated subjects, but Charles was far too gracious to say so directly. It spoke very well of him that he should be so kind toward one who was well known to be wanting in most accomplishments and, if truth be told, in his character as well.

"Did you see that?" He shaded his eyes as he peered off into a clump of fragrant hawthorn bushes that marked the border of Lady Russell's gardens at Kellynch Cottage.

"What did you see?"

He rubbed his eyes with thumb and forefinger. "It must have been nothing, but for a moment I thought I saw a very large, brightly-colored bird."

"There are some bright wrens that frequent the garden."

"This was far larger than any wren, larger than a swan even. No matter, I am sure my eyes were just playing tricks on me. With all the blossoms around us, I am certain it was simply a clump of flowers swaying in the wind."

"You must be correct." She stooped to smell a cluster of purple bee balm—spicy, oregano with hints of mint and thyme—braving the buzzing bees surrounding it. "I am sorry to hear your mother is downhearted on his behalf, though."

"To be honest, I do not expect it to improve. Papa has been talking of sending him into the navy."

Who knew a lump so large could rise so quickly in one's throat? "The navy?"

"What else is to be done with him? He must have some sort of profession. If he cannot learn classical languages, then he will not make it through university. So, he can be neither a vicar nor a barrister." His voice turned cynical. "I suppose Father could try to purchase him a commission and send him into the regulars."

Anne winced.

"Clearly you understand how bad an idea that is."

"I do not mean to speak ill of your brother, but yes, I can understand your father's reluctance."

"So, then what else is to be done with him? Father cannot, will not, support him all of his life, especially in the life of some sort of a dandy who is good for nothing and no one." His heavy boots fell, hard and regular, along the gravel.

But not nearly as harsh as his father's judgments would fall. The senior Mr. Musgrove had some very definite opinions of foppish young men who strutted like peacocks and spent money not their own. One of the few very strong opinions he held. No son of his would ever resemble "one of those."

"So, then I expect, he is for the navy." Charles clasped his hands behind his back, his head slightly bowed.

Anne swallowed hard. She had to say something, but her voice faltered. "I thought that life could be quite harsh. Surely harsher than school could be."

"Yes, yes, it is. But it is the making of many young men. Father hopes it will be the making of Dick."

If it was not his undoing first. But that was impolitic to say.

"I think Mother is very glad that the decision is not hers to make. She is happy to leave the raising of her sons to Father. Selecting a school for my sisters was taxing enough for her."

Anne chuckled. Mrs. Musgrove disliked decisions only slightly less than Father disliked inferior company.

"My father has been turning more and more of the business of the estate over to me." Charles kicked at a clod of dirt into a clump of bee balm. Bees scattered away from the swaying stalks.

He seemed to be hoping she would say something? But what was he looking for? "How do you find the activity?"

His posture straightened, and his voice turned lighter. "Actually, quite invigorating. I did not expect it to be so, but in truth, I like it very well."

"Then I am happy for you. It is fortunate to be able to sample one's destiny and find it agreeable."

He turned to her and looked straight into her eyes,

something he almost never did. "You say the most curious things, Miss Elliot." The corners of his lips turned up. Was he amused with her or was he laughing at her? The distinction was small but significant. "Has anyone told you that before?"

"No not at all." But then again, no one listened to her in the first place, so why would they?

He shrugged and trundled on. "I have been giving a great deal of thought to the future recently."

"And what have you concluded?"

"That it is time for you to change your name."

"I beg your pardon."

"I need a wife."

Anne stopped so suddenly she nearly tripped. "A wife?"

He caught her elbow and steadied her for a brief moment. "Indeed, a wife. It is the done thing, you know. A man cannot have a household without one. Well I suppose he could, with a sister or housekeeper or some such, but it is hardly the same and hardly what I have envisioned for myself."

"I see."

"Do you?"

She edged back a mite.

He took a half step closer. "Perhaps you do not, Miss Anne. I would very much like you to be my wife."

"Oh." Her eyes grew wide and her jaw dropped before she could properly school her expression. Was that how he thought one made an offer of marriage? Wentworth had—

"Oh? I am not sure what sort of an answer that is."

"I ... you must forgive me, but your question has

taken me completely by surprise." By its complete lack of feeling and finesse.

"Has it? I was certain you would have been anticipating it by now." His eyebrows rose high enough to hide under the brim of his hat.

She pressed a hand to her chest to quell the rising breathlessness. "I am afraid I am quite unprepared." At least that much was true.

"I see. Does this mean you do not have an answer for me?"

"Pray forgive me, but I believe I must have some little time to consider." It was the proper thing to do, to give a question proper consideration before making an answer, was it not? Certainly, that would soften the blow when she—

Yes, consider it.

"That seems reasonable enough." He nodded as though trying to convince himself. "You know my home and what I am heir to. You know my family, so I suppose there is little you have further need to discover. So then, it should not take you very long."

"Indeed, I cannot think of anything more I need to know. I just need time to think." Why was her heart pounding so hard?

Yes, think, take time to think.

"Shall I leave you to do so then? Perhaps call on you in a few days to receive your answer?" He cocked his head with a look of vague expectation.

"Yes, I think that would do." She pressed her pounding temples. The burgeoning headache threatened to be a spectacular one.

"Very well then. I shall see you on Friday." He tipped his hat and sauntered away.

How odd that he should not have even offered to

walk her back to the house. Wentworth had done as much when he had taken her by surprise with his— dare she describe it—utterly romantic offer. The eloquence and the feelings he professed—so far beyond what staid Charles was ever likely to experience or admit to.

She watched him until he disappeared among the blossoms and bushes. Charles Musgrove had just made her an offer of marriage.

An offer of marriage.

Tall flowers leaned toward her as though they wished to offer advice. She brushed them aside. No, she would not be persuaded this time. She would consult only her own heart and mind and make the decision for herself alone.

She pressed her temples hard and turned back toward the house. Perhaps she would lie down. That might ease the thundering in her skull.

A very large, colorful bird launched from the bushes nearby, cawing as it went. What kind of a fancy fowl was that? What was it doing out in the garden? Was that the bird Charles thought he had seen? Maybe, when she felt a little less horrid, she would talk with the gamekeeper; he might know something.

An hour or so in bed and her headache had subsided, but that hardly meant she felt well. How could one possibly feel well when wrestling with such a question?

Anne took special care in dressing for dinner. She donned a rose-colored sprigged lawn gown. Elizabeth has discarded it after several seasons as no longer fashionable enough. The cut and the shade suited

Anne well, though, and a set of fresh ribbons and new puffed sleeves made it quite her own. Most importantly, Elizabeth seemed to find it a compliment that Anne wore it—or maybe she thought something entirely different, but it did lift her mood to see Anne in it. Anything to make dinnertime conversation easier was to be sought after, especially tonight when there were so many things of which she could not speak.

Dinner was served at a fashionable hour: an hour after sundown just as it always was. What matter that they were in the country? Keeping fashionable hours ensured a baronet would be seen to be living like a baronet. It also required an excessive use of candles—wax, not tallow of course—and many platters of food prepared for just the four of them. No matter that most of it would go toward lining Cook's pocket when she sold the leavings from the kitchen door.

Such a waste. Not the sort of thing that happened when Mama was alive. Then there was moderation and economy at Kellynch.

The hair on the back of Anne's neck rose. The last time she had suggested that a little economy would hardly be felt, Father carried on as though she had asked him to go begging in the street. The question of who was seeing their private dinners and how anyone would know they were living as a proper baronet's family did never received an answer.

It was not a conversation worth repeating. Ever.

Anne peeked into the drawing room—empty. How kind of Father and Elizabeth to decide not to wait for her in the sitting room as polite company did. Dare one suggest that it might be what a proper baronet's family would do? No, one did not dare say it, but she might think it rather loudly.

She set out for the small dining room, slippers whispering along the long marble corridor, and slipped into her seat at the oblong dining table as silverware clinked on dinner china. Her stomach pinched uneasily at the smells of the different platters vying with one another for attention. Broiled trout and stewed apples really did not belong side-by-side at the table.

At least Father had agreed to use the small dining room. Yes, it left them with eight empty places, but that was better than twenty empty chairs in the large dining room. A silver candelabra glittered at each of the table's corners with two large matching candlesticks in the middle of the table. There was nearly enough light to sew by! Flickering light glittered off the mirrors hanging over the mahogany sideboards against the long walls. Dancing shadows cast by empty chairs cavorted amongst the many serving dishes on the table. Were those empty chairs filled by ghosts of departed generations of Elliots?

"How good of you to finally join us Anne. I was beginning to think we would be eating without you." Mary, sitting across the table from Anne, tucked her napkin in her lap. Her complexion turned ruddy in the candlelight. That, with her rounded shoulders and tendency to carry herself as rather short and dumpy though not particularly heavy—almost as though to set herself apart from Elizabeth's elegant columnar figure—almost invariably drew a sour remark from Father. Not surprisingly, dinnertime generally saw her ill-tempered.

"There is no need to be rude. I am sure Anne had her reasons." Elizabeth, presiding at the head of the table, tipped her head toward Anne, but her green eyes were still narrow and sharp, rather like her shoulders and elbows. Just a mite too sharp to be willowy and elegant. Her leaf-green silk dinner gown matched her eyes.

"Pray do forgive me. I have had a frightful headache," Anne muttered to her plate—white with a wide red border, a script initial "E" in a lozenge at the top, and a gilt band around the edge. Not that anyone would particularly care why she had been late. Was that a good thing or not?

Likely, it was a good thing. As pleasing as it might be to be taken notice of, the only conversation she wanted to have was definitely not something to share in this company. Or perhaps any. Was there anyone she could discuss such a thing with?

"You are not the only one who has had a headache," Mary muttered as she tore a bit from her roll.

Father stood to carve the joint, tall and straight in his finely tailored black suit. His hair was arranged in the latest style, something with Caesar in the name, if she recalled correctly. He would be appalled to know she had forgotten the name.

He really was a well-looking man, certainly well enough looking to have found a new wife by now. Especially considering his title and lands. That he had not spoke volumes; volumes that Anne would not—should not—ponder on.

Servants took the carved mutton to the ladies' plates. They would not have had so far to go had Father permitted them to all sit at one end of the table. But no, he would not give up his honored position at the foot nor insist that Elizabeth relinquish hers.

Nor would he renounce the need for conversation,

so they all had to speak loudly—impolitely one might argue—in order to be heard. Was it possible that Father was becoming hard of hearing? No, she would not broach that possibility, definitely not.

Anne forced a pleasant expression on her face. Good thing that no one would be looking closely enough to see through her thin disguise. It was for the best that she was rarely required to actually speak.

"Have you given more thought to a Season in London, Father?" Elizabeth cut a tiny bite from her meat.

"I have, I have, but I am not sure it is the correct move to make just now." Father took a large sip of wine.

Elizabeth's face knotted, but she drew a deep breath. Thank heavens she had long since given up petulant tantrums in favor of more ladylike behavior. "Remember, Lady Russell suggested that it would be most advantageous. She assures me that we would be welcomed into the most appropriate circles. Circles in which there are many suitable young men."

Men with titles and connections, looking for women with connections and fortunes.

"There is that, to be sure. But the issue of who would make introductions remains unsettled and of grave concern." Why did it sound like a threat to the empire when Father said it?

"I have hardly been able to lift my head all day, and none of you has asked after me." Mary pushed mutton around her plate, shoulders slumped. Father must be pondering very hard indeed not to reprimand her for her posture.

Anne forced herself not to roll her eyes. "I had no idea you were feeling poorly—"

"Do we not know several families who are residing in London during the Season?" Elizabeth turned her face away from Mary's side of the table.

"We do, but none who are as distinguished as our cousins, the Dalrymples. They do not intend to be in London this Season. We should not risk bad connections, you know. It would be a sad thing for any of you girls to expose the Elliot name to low connections, especially you, my dear."

Elizabeth blushed prettily. "Do you know what keeps them from London?"

"Perhaps their daughter is ill, as surely I am. I am certain I should see a surgeon or at least the apothecary."

"I am certain one of Mama's teas will set you to rights." Anne leaned toward Mary. "Tell me more of what is troubling you. I am certain I can make you something to help."

"I am not entirely certain, though I thought I heard something about his gout. Nasty disagreeable stuff that is." Father cut a large piece of meat and chewed thoughtfully.

"That would probably limit the socializing they could do even if they were to visit town for the Season."

"I do not want any of your teas." Mary hissed over her plate, turning her shoulder to Anne.

"Then what do you want?"

"Besides, I think there may be another way for you to meet a suitable young man." Father smiled, a little smug and self-satisfied. "In fact, we are expecting a visit from such a person later this summer."

"A visit? Who is coming?" Elizabeth's features brightened.

"If we have a visitor, I shall need my dresses mended. That is what I hoped to do today and could not because of my headache."

Anne's stomach knotted. How soon would she have to start preparing the house for a guest?

"Mr. William Elliot, heir presumptive to Kellynch, is coming to see us at the beginning of September."

"That is not very much time. I will need to have a new dress made." Elizabeth plucked at her sleeves. Had she forgotten that particular gown was less than six months old?

"I do not suppose I am to have a new gown, though it would be very nice. Mine should at least be mended. Anne, you will help me, will you not?" Mary's tone made it clear—it was not a question.

"Of course, you shall have a new gown, probably two, just to be certain. We must make the most of the opportunity," Father said.

Elizabeth beamed and nodded. It must be pleasant to receive more than one asked for.

"Anne? Are you listening? You will help me with my gowns, yes?"

Something snapped, like a corset lace breaking, and everything seemed to come loose and unraveled. Anne set down her fork and knife and stared at Mary. "No, I will not."

"What do you mean you will not?"

Anne winced. Usually, she would have agreed, merely to make Mary happy and stop her from complaining. But not today. How could she comfort Mary and still keep inside all those things she could not possibly speak aloud?

"What do you mean you will not help me?" Mary's voice became a whine, an invisible hand reaching out to strangle her.

Anne clutched edge of her seat and fought for breath.

"Anne ... Anne, are you listening to me?" Mary rapped the table.

Anne stood. "Pray excuse me."

"This is most unusual." Father cleared his throat.

Elizabeth glowered at Anne. "It would be pleasing to have a fourth for dinner."

"Perhaps tomorrow. Pray excuse me." Anne curtsied and hurried upstairs to her chambers.

Mary would be quite put out; she would probably keep to her bed all the next day and blame it on Anne. Tonight, it would be Mary's problem, not hers.

She would likely feel guilty for it, but that would wait for morning. Tonight, she needed—and would have—quiet and solitude.

4
Chapter

SHE CLOSED HER door behind her and turned the key. No, not even servants were welcome tonight. Unlike her sisters, she was perfectly capable of attending the fire, turning down her bedclothes and undressing without a maid. Father would call it a foolish sentiment, but it was hers. For the moment, she would embrace it with all that she had as proof she was capable of making a decision and holding to it, unpopular though it might be.

Perhaps it was stupid, but she would draw strength where she could. She had to make a decision, and she had to do it quickly—before the weight of it suffocated her.

Why had she bothered to go downstairs for dinner at all? It was not as though she had expected sympathy or any sort of advice. Habit, force of habit, that was the only reason and clearly not a good one.

She pressed her back to the paneled door and slowly slid to the polished wood floor. How odd the room looked from this vantage point. Two stubby candles in pewter candlesticks on either end of the mantel lit the room with just enough light, but no more. Shadows danced on the wall behind the four-poster bed, reaching the chest of drawers on the near wall and the small round table and overstuffed burgundy armchair near the window opposite her. If only the shadows had answers to offer. The faint scent of beeswax and old flowers hung in the air. The soft green walls yellowed in the candlelight making her room feel tired and aged.

Drawing her knees to her chest she hid her face in her hands. Her chest tightened until she could hardly breathe, her eyes burning. Tears should have followed. It would have been a relief if they had, but no, they too, were a comfort to be denied her.

She was alone.

It had been that way so long now, it felt normal, even right most of the time. Since Elizabeth had taken over the household, Anne eschewed seeking out the mistress of the house for anything resembling comfort or wisdom. Elizabeth had none to give. There was no point in becoming upset about that; one could not squeeze blood from a stone.

Self-sufficiency proved hard at times and lonely almost always. Doubly so right now.

There had been only one to whom she could have turned who would have understood and been able to help her make sense of the churning confusion. The one who tried to stand in that stead now, Lady Russell, would certainly have been willing to try … no that was not going to happen.

Not again.

She did not resent—or at least she thought she did not resent—Lady Russell for her advice two—now it was nearly three—years ago. No! What point was there in rehashing it yet again?

Wentworth's career and future—he had no fortune and no sure promise of one. The casualty rate of naval men was hardly a secret. Once she left her father's house, there was no certainty that Father would have her back, much less any children who might come with her, should something befall her husband. Not that Lady Russell had said as much directly, but she did hint at it rather strongly, and sadly, it was a just point.

Yet, looking back on it now, just a few years later, different conclusions seemed more appropriate: little in life was certain, and while fortune and security were good things, perhaps, just perhaps, those were not the only ones to be considered. There was a great deal to be said for warm affections and attachments that were sure.

A very great deal.

Without a doubt, Lady Russell would not have agreed, and she would have found a thousand reasons to support her point. So, that conversation, like so many others, would never happen.

Anne lifted her head and bounced it off the door with a dull thud. It hurt, but in a sort of clarifying way—did that even make sense or was she finally going daft?

She pushed up from the floor and forced her feet into motion. Eight steps across the room took her to the upholstered chair near the window whose rose-and-vine printed curtains were now drawn against the evening chill. She curled up in the chair, arms around her legs, rested her chin on her knees, and watched the dancing shadows.

Lady Russell and her opinions were not her concern right now. Charles Musgrove was.

What was one to do with one Charles Musgrove?

Oh, Charles.

He was an excellent young man to be sure. Steady, kind, of unquestionable character. And his family—such delights! His mother and sisters all excellent company and so welcoming of her—more so than her own were. It was tempting to accept him just on the basis of his relations who seemed to relish her company. What a change that would be to Kellynch.

The corner of her lips lifted. To enjoy the companionship of a mother again, her advice, her tutelage, her doting. Her throat grew too tight for breath. What would Mama think of that?

One did not marry a man for such reasons.

No, perhaps some did, but it hardly seemed like a good idea.

There was Elizabeth to consider. She would not be pleased. Though she had no designs on Charles herself, to be sure, the Musgrove family was not nearly high enough for her liking. She might consider it a very hard thing to have such low connections thrust upon her.

Moreover, the eldest daughter should marry first. That was how it was done and how it would be done in a proper family like the Elliots. Then again, Elizabeth had not "taken" despite being out several years. Did that not give her sisters, now out themselves, the right to marry if an offer came to them? That, too, was how it was done in proper families.

The hair on the back of Anne's neck stood on end. Oh, Elizabeth would not like to hear that.

Even with Elizabeth's censure, Father would not disapprove. Uppercross, the Musgrove family lands, were not as extensive as Kellynch, but they were a close second in the county. The Musgroves were by no means poor. The family did not have a title, but only Elizabeth had any right to expect to marry into such rarified company. Surely Father would not care if her own husband was a Mister or a Sir. He would probably be pleased just to have her safely married off and entered into the *Baronetage*, and not to be thought of after that.

Was that thought harsh or merely realistic?

In truth, there was no valid reason to refuse. Charles was companionable enough; they could expect to live in harmony and warmth. It was more than many young women in her circumstance could anticipate.

She laced her hands behind her head and huddled into herself.

It should be enough. It should be and for more reasons than the assets of his home, his family and his fortune. Charles was a good sort of man. A kind man, a regular sort of dependable man.

A dull man with common interests and pursuits. He had little curiosity, no sense of adventure, no desire for more than what he already knew and had. He was boring.

Very boring.

But his fortune and his future were secure and she would remain near to her family home.

Those were the very qualities that Wentworth did not have in his favor when he had made her an offer of marriage … and ruined her for any other.

She stood and paced the room. Once around, twice, thrice. That was it—this was not about Charles at all. It was about Wentworth!

Heavens above! It should not be.

But it was.

Something like cool water—perhaps relief or was it clarity?—spread from the top of her head, slowly toward her feet.

Of course, the answer was so obvious and clear.

Charles was not enough, not nearly enough. He had not Wentworth's wit, his charm, his intelligence, his active mind and interests.

Charles Musgrove was not a stupid man, but he was staid and predictable … and dull. In his presence, she was secure in knowing, at least most of the time, precisely what he would say and do. And she hated it.

Wentworth never bowed to such predictability, but yet, she always felt safe; his character would never permit harm to come to her. While Charles was hardly a danger to her, he had not Wentworth's protective nature.

And after years in Father's house, to know she might be protected and—dare she say it—cherished—yes! That was what she desired above all else. But it was something Charles would—could—never do. Was it worth settling for that to merely escape Father's household?

Her heart hammered so hard she could barely hear her own thoughts. But there it was, the whisper she had refused to acknowledge for so long. Wentworth had loved her. He loved her.

Love, a silly, frivolous emotion that had little place in the business of marriage.

Charles did not. Charles liked her, esteemed her. Found her comfortable and easy—what was it Lady Russell had called her? Pretty enough, well-connected and convenient? No, Charles had not said that, but it certainly sounded like something he would say.

Still, he did not love her. He might grow to love her, but then again, he might not.

She had been loved once and turned aside from it. Settling for less than that now was simply and utterly impossible. What more was there to say?

As good and kind as Charles was, she would have to disappoint him.

It would be a difficult conversation. But not more awful—and far more correct—than telling Wentworth the same thing.

And she would not mention it to Lady Russell until all was said and done.

The following morning, Anne rose early and donned a comfortable roller-printed morning gown, a dark green and puce striped affair. Elizabeth had stripped it of its fancy trims—they now adorned one of her walking dresses—and passed it to Anne. Without all the fuss, it was much prettier and more wearable now, another sentiment probably best kept to herself.

She made her way to the sunny morning room, Mama's commonplace book tucked under her arm. A maid bustled in with the tall white-and-rose-vine patterned chocolate pot—it was not the sort of morning for tea—and whisked it hard with the chocolate mill, raising a lovely froth. Anne set a chocolate cup in its railed saucer, and the maid filled it, fragrant, spicy vapors rising from the froth. Lovely notes of nutmeg and a hint of chili.

Balancing the lid on the cup, she carefully made her way to the chair nearest the windows. There she would enjoy the quiet room, the warmth of the morning sun and pretending to read Mama's commonplace book over her morning chocolate. Acting as though everything were normal might just tide her through until everything became normal again.

Sky-blue paper hangings with fluffy white clouds and odd-looking small birds decorated the wall, interrupted in places by Mama's watercolor landscapes—and Elizabeth's which stood out in unfavorable comparison. None of the five empty places around the small round morning table would likely be filled before she left. Still too early for the rest of the family. A mite lonely with only the company of the rather plain dark oak table, chairs and sideboards, but Mama had decorated this room to her simple and cozy tastes. In her lingering presence, any real loneliness faded away.

What would Mama say to her current dilemma? Doubtless, she would agree that Anne should not delay delivering her news to Charles. But he did not intend to revisit Kellynch until Friday, and calling upon him at Uppercross was hardly proper.

How was she to tolerate the weight of her answer that long? Was there not some way to make that meeting happen sooner?

"Miss Anne?" Mrs. Trent, the housekeeper, curtsied at the doorway. "Lady Russell just arrived for you."

"Lady Russell?" It was awfully early for her to call. Their acquaintance was such that it was not improper, but still, she was hardly apt to visit before noon.

Something was not right. "I will see her in the parlor. Prepare a cup of chocolate for her. You know the way she prefers it." Anne tucked her book under one arm and picked up her chocolate in the other hand. The cup rattled against the saucer rails, clinking in time with Anne's pounding heart.

She arrived in the parlor just ahead of Lady Russell and opened the double doors to the light and airy, pale yellow room, her slippers padding softly along the sand-colored tile. A wall of tall windows looked out over Mama's favorite garden. All the furniture—pale oak, upholstered in tones of gold and orange—had been arranged to encourage one to look out over the bevy of blossoms, making it feel like an extension of the garden itself. Floral paintings and vases and bowls of fresh, sweet flowers that perfumed the air only reinforced the sensation.

"I hope I have not caught you at a bad moment, my dear." Lady Russell, clad in her trademark blue, strode in—such a long, unusual gait for a lady—and settled on her favorite rust colored chair, the plump overstuffed one nearest the window. Odd, how she always liked to sit near a window, particularly an open one, and the way she sat was rather reminiscent of a bird on a nest. It was probably not complimentary to think that.

"No, no, not at all." Anne pulled a small lyre-back chair near Lady Russell.

"You look troubled. Is there something with which I might be able to help you?" Lady Russell cocked her head just so, the large feather on her hat bobbing against her forehead. Such an odd little habit she had, decidedly wren-like, especially when one considered how her dark eyes glittered in the sunlight.

"Not really. I have come to a decision, and I am quite content in it. There are just some situations for which no decision, even the right one, feels very good." Anne sipped her chocolate—too much nutmeg and it could do with a touch more chili—and gazed at the colorful little birds diving and weaving amongst the garden blossoms—so bright and gay. Perhaps that answer would be enough.

"What sort of decision have you been wrestling with? It sounds like a very serious one."

"Truly it is nothing. I have already satisfied myself. You need not be worried."

Lady Russell leaned in close and touched Anne's hand. "But I am worried, most concerned in fact. As your friend and your departed mother's, it is my duty to try and help you in any way I can."

"I know that. You have always been a very great support to me." Though not one that had always been correct.

"Then allow me to support you now."

"I have made my decision. There is no need to discuss it." Anne set her chocolate cup firmly into its railed saucer that balanced on her lap.

"At the very least then, tell me what you have decided." There was an odd tone in Lady Russell's voice. Whispery and grating, like rubbing sand across one's face.

Tell her! Tell her!

Anne sighed. She would know soon enough, so what point in obfuscating? "I was made an offer of marriage."

"Marriage? By whom?" Her eyes grew wide, feigning surprise. How kind of her.

"How many young men do I know?"

"Charles Musgrove, as I expected?" Lady Russell bit her lip. Why was she playing this game? "What was your decision?"

Anne nodded and shifted her gaze to the window, away from Lady Russell's piercing eyes. "I do not expect to be changing my name anytime soon."

"You will reject him?" Now she sounded genuinely shocked. Her knee knocked against the small table, rattling her chocolate cup.

"Indeed, I shall. I am quite content with my decision—"

"How can you be? Why on earth would you reject him?" There was that peculiar sound again, stabbing at her ears like a sharp quill.

You are making a mistake!

Anne pressed her palms to the side of her head. "I have weighed it all out very carefully. I am quite certain it is the right thing to do."

"I am quite certain it is not." Lady Russell huffed and sat up very straight, her chest puffing out just a bit, rather like Father's when he was making a point.

"Pray excuse me. Whatever do you mean?" Anne gripped the sides of her chair.

"He is an excellent young man. His fortune is secure; his connections are good; his reputation first-rate. And you would be settled within such an easy distance of Kellynch. We might continue as we always have with one another. What more does a young man need to convince you?"

"I notice that you do not ask: what does a young woman need? I am not certain that his offer is enough."

"Of course, it is." Lady Russell bobbed her head as though that settled the matter.

"He is a good sort of man to be sure, but I do not think he is what I want."

"How would you know what you want? He is an excellent match."

Accept him.

Anne ducked her head and shook it sharply against the aching buzzing in her temples that grew sharper at Lady Russell's every word. "He may be, but I hope for more than he can give me."

"You are being foolish. How many more chances to settle well do you think you will have?" Lady Russell's eyes narrowed. "You are comparing him to Wentworth."

"And if I am? I do not think it is a bad thing. He was an admirable—"

"Utter foolishness." She waved her hand in a great sweeping gesture, dismissing the very notion. "Truly it is, and you must stop. I cannot permit you make this sort of mistake. I care for you too much."

Anne placed her chocolate cup on the nearby little square table slowly, deliberately. "I am two and twenty, not a child. I am very well able to make a good decision. I would appreciate it—"

Lady Russell leaned forward and stared intently into Anne's eyes. "I am sure it seems that way to you. But you must trust me. In this matter there are things I understand that you do not. You must listen to me."

Listen to me. Listen to me. Listen!

The words echoed over and over in Anne's skull, ricocheting like billiard balls from one side to the other and back again. Clacking and rattling each time they struck an obstacle, threatening to wear down her resolve. She bowed her head, collapsing into her lap, cradling her head in her arms.

"Anne, what is wrong?" Lady Russell stood over her. "Are you unwell?"

"My head! My head feels like it is about to shatter. Pray excuse me. I must go to my room." Anne sprang to her feet, unsteady and dizzy.

"I will take you. You should not be alone." Lady Russell reached for her.

"No, no. I must be alone right now. I do not think I can tolerate even the sound of another person breathing!" Anne pelted from the room as fast as her shaky legs would take her.

At the grand stairs, the razor's edge of the pain seemed to fade. Not that she felt well, not by any means. But the initial urge to cast up her accounts had passed and perhaps, just perhaps, she would be able to make it to her room without calling for assistance.

5
Chapter

ANNE'S HEADACHE PERSISTED the entire night and continued for the next two days. Blinding, nauseating pain encompassed her entire being, subsiding at just the moment that flinging herself from her window to the garden below seemed like a very good idea. Thankfully, that urge passed with the worst of the pain. Still though, she spent two more days in bed recovering from the experience, naturally missing Charles Musgrove's call.

Mary said he sent his well wishes and would return in a few more days for an interview with her. Once Anne felt a little stronger, no doubt she would find missing the interview extremely vexing. But for now, simply standing up and looking into the sunshine without knives shooting through her skull were pleasures not to be underestimated. Perhaps that was a little dramatic. It did sound like something Mary would say. But was it wrong to express oneself that way when it was entirely true?

After five days of confinement, Anne craved sunshine and fresh air even more than food and drink. Finally feeling strong enough for both, she donned a plain pink muslin morning dress, slipped into the kitchen for a slice of bread and cheese, and made her way to her mother's garden behind the house.

Perfectly lovely sunbeams kissed her skin with warmth, reminding her of the pleasure of being alive. She chuckled. There was that dramatic streak coming out again, but as long as she kept it to herself, surely the indulgence was not so bad.

Near the overflowing white peony blooms with their heady perfume, the air hummed with the determined buzz of the local bees, their pulsing thrum more a feeling than a sound. She pressed her temples—something was off. The garden was familiar but somehow different.

It made no sense.

Perchance her eyes were weary from the days in her darkened room, but still, things looked different, just a little, like a person sitting for a silhouette who kept moving just a mite. Right and not right, rapidly alternating by moments. The garden sounded different too, but no word aptly described how—maybe brighter, more in focus? But those were words that described sight, not sound.

Lingering effects of the headache, perhaps? No doubt they would pass.

Anne continued along the little trail between the peonies that grew narrower as it went. How comfortably intimate the embrace of the flowers. Heavy perfume—a sweet interweaving of jasmine, rose and gillyflower—filled the air.

A rabbit trail opened up to the left. She stopped and peered down the narrow opening. Sometimes, when she was lucky, she could see the fuzzy little dears looking back at her with their bright eyes and long ears. Yes, there was one!

She crouched and leaned onto her heels. If she were very quiet, it might stay a bit and allow her to watch. It turned to look at her. Wait—what? No …

Her eyes lost focus, and the image of the rabbit melted away like butter in a hot pan. The creature that now stared back at her—what was it?

Fangs. It had fangs.

A shudder began at the back of her neck and snaked down her spine.

About the size of a large rabbit, its scaly hide was a sort of brown-green that blended in with the garden plants. The tip of its long tail flicked warily, and a substantial frill flared up behind its head.

"What are you?" Anne whispered.

"I am a rabbit in the garden." It spoke in a painful, raspy odd voice. Not the sort of voice a rabbit should have, if a rabbit should have the power of speech.

"No, you are definitely not a rabbit. What are you?"

Its tail slapped the ground. "Excuse me, but you are quite rude! Clearly, the question is 'who am I' not 'what.' I am Beebalm, and I am a puck, you stupid girl." The voice, different now, was staccato, breathy, and the tiniest bit cold.

Anne fell back to sit hard on the ground, catching herself with her palms. No, it was not possible. The creature could not have spoken to her. "What is a puck?"

Why was she even talking to it?

The creature's wide lacy frill fluttered open, and it hissed, sharp teeth bared. Anne scrabbled back.

"Do you know nothing? I am a dragon." It stomped its left front foot. Long dark claws tore at the ground.

"You are very small for a dragon. I thought they were very large." And that they were only myths.

"You are a stupid girl. I had hoped for better from you. You really ought to apply yourself to learning something useful before you speak. Yes, you ought." The creature turned on its tail and hopped into the dense flowerbeds, snorting as it disappeared.

Anne rubbed the dusty heels of her hands into her eyes. She must be seeing things. And hearing them, too. Had she just been scolded by a miniature dragon? That headache had truly affected her; that was the only possible explanation.

It was not a good sign, not at all.

She pushed herself back to her feet, a bit light-headed and wobbly. Best return to the house, no doubt she was trying to do too much. A bit more rest; that would set things to right.

Slowly, deliberately, she forced one foot in front of the other, gravel crunching under her half-boots, dusty skirts swishing around her ankles. There, she was feeling better already. As she turned down the path toward the house, the head shepherd's dog trotted toward her.

Thick and stocky and covered with rich brown and white fur, he woofed at her, smiling his unselfconscious canine smile. He sat, panting, and waited for his customary scratch under the chin. Thank heavens, a creature who would not talk back to her!

"Such a fine fellow." She scratched his scaly neck.

Scaly?

Cold prickles coursed down her neck and shoulders as she edged back and peered at the sheepdog. Like the rabbit, the dog-form liquefied and sloughed away, revealing a decidedly medieval dragon-like creature the size and shape of the dog that been there before.

Its hind leg scratched behind its small pointed ear with long dangerous-looking talons. "Do not look at me so curiously. I am the dog you have always known." The voice was whispery-painful, like the sounds she had heard in her last conversation with Lady Russell.

"No, not at all. You look nothing like a dog at all. What has happened to you?" Anne drove the heels of her hands into her temples and cast about—were there more of these creatures in the bushes?

It stood and wagged its long thick tail exactly as the dog had, the sun glinting off the almost-white and brown spotted scales on its back. Triangular ears, pinkish white in the center, pricked toward her. "So, it has happened at last. Good on you, Miss. Good on you. It is about time there is a proper Keeper for these lands." The voice changed to something no longer painful; rich and a bit rough, a voice she could have imagined belonging to a large dog.

"Keeper? I do not know what you are talking about. I do not know why you are talking at all."

"I think the real question here is not why I am talking, but why you have only just started to hear me? I declare it an odd thing to take so long to grow into one's hearing."

"You have been talking all this time?" Her mouth went dry.

"Yes, but not to you of course, except to persuade you that I was the dog you used to see." The creature yawned—what a huge mouth! Fangs! And those teeth—so many, so sharp ...

"But why would you do that?"

"If you think yourself shocked now, talking to a dragon, how much more would you be to see one and not be able to talk to him? You would think me some sort of frightful beast." He sat back down and cocked his head at her in an expression she had often seen the sheepdog use.

"I suppose that makes sense." At least it seemed to, considering that this situation that made no sense at all.

"Of course, it does. Dragons are eminently sensible." His thick tail swished along the pebbles.

"I will have to take your word on it."

"Your mother often did."

"You knew my mother?" Her knees melted beneath her, and she sagged to the ground, sharp gravel biting into her palm.

"Naturally. She knew all of us by name."

"All of you? You have a name?"

"Of course, we do! We are not uncivilized. I am Shelby." Was he laughing at her as he bent his front legs and bowed his head?

She stood and struggled through an artless curtsy—why was hard to say—more reflex than anything else. "I ... I am pleased to make your acquaintance." Did she just say that to a creature who called itself a dragon? A dragon!

"You remind me of your mother. Once we were acquainted, she proved quite hospitable." He lifted his nose and sniffed the air. "Must get back to the sheep." He trotted away as though nothing unusual at all had taken place.

She stared after him. Pray let him turn back into a dog.

But he did not.

Oh, for a nearby bench! How could one remain standing after such an encounter? There, under the white lattice gazebo, a small iron bench. She staggered there as quickly as her feeble knees could take her.

Surely her head should be hurting now, but it did not. Why?

She sat, hunched over her lap, fingertips pressed hard to her temples. There was some natural explanation for these events. Surely there was.

Perhaps one—but not a pleasing one. She must be going mad—stark mad! Bedlam should be her home soon! What else could it be?

That would be Father's undoing! A daughter in Bedlam—it might even kill him.

"You see, you see!" A voice—not another voice!—twittered above her.

She craned her neck and peered into the bright blue sky, wishing, praying to see the pretty little wrens—the ones Mother and Lady Russell used to talk to—that frequented the garden. Two colorful creatures circled above her. At first glance, they seemed to be small birds, but she squinted and they became scaly, lizardy creatures: four-legged, with fluffy not-quite-feathers, but not-quite-scales either, rendering them in bright rainbow shades.

The larger one dipped down close to her. "The

daughter of the house hears us now! She hears! I am sure of it."

"But what does it mean? Does any know her character, her motives?" The smaller one perched on the topmost rail of the gazebo.

"Who can tell, she has no signet of the Order, no sign that she is our friend." The large one swooped through the lattice, in and out of the gazebo's domed top.

"Then I shall not stay, not until there is some sign she is trustworthy."

The two little birds—no creatures; could it be more dragons?—zipped off into the garden and disappeared among the flowers.

No! No! Not the birds, too. Enough! Enough!

She dragged herself back into the house and shut the front door hard, pressing her back against the door lest any more dragon-creatures try to make their way in. None appeared from the flowers in the tall vase on the hall table or peeked out from behind the Elliot family portraits on the opposite wall. Thank heavens! She dragged in a long, ragged breath.

Sharp footsteps rang out in the front hall, coming closer. She most certainly did not need to be seen, her hair disheveled and covered in dirt.

"Anne? Anne? What is wrong with you? You look a fright." Father, hands firmly clasped behind his back, stared at her with more condemnation than concern. His suit, his shoes, the arrangement of his hair were, as always, impeccable.

"I am quite unwell. I am seeing things and hearing things that simply cannot be." She braced for his rebuke.

His eyes narrowed, and his forehead wrinkled—an

expression his vanity usually obviated. "What sorts of things?"

"Does it really matter?" She pushed stray hairs back from her forehead.

"It does, I am afraid. What sorts of things?" He waved for her to follow him as he walked down the corridor toward his study, hands clasped tight behind his back, footsteps hushed by the thick carpet.

How could he ask her to walk at such a time? "It sounds like some sort of fairy story. Whilst I was in the garden, I am quite certain that animals there talked to me."

Why did he not look more surprised? "Go on." He ushered her into his office and shut the door rather firmly.

The room was stark and neat, curtains and carpet in stripes of ivory, gold, and blue. The wall to the left of the door boasted a pair of large bookcases that flanked Father's desk. The opposite wall held the fireplace, fronted by several large navy-blue arm-chairs. Between were cabinets and shelves holding the usual sorts of things men appreciated in their bookrooms.

"A rabbit, who said she knew Mama. A shepherd's dog and a pair of birds. They all spoke to me." She clutched the back of the wooden chair nearest the desk.

Father tut-tutted under his breath. "Are you certain it was a rabbit?"

"No, not exactly.

He dropped into the large chair behind his grand mahogany desk and looked her square in the eyes. "Stop dithering about, and tell me the whole thing."

"I thought it was a rabbit at first, but as I watched,

it changed into something else. Something I have never seen before. With scales and fangs. It called itself a puck, which it said was a kind of dragon. The dog did the same, but it looked like a small dragon from a fairy story. And the birds that flew over me. I could hardly see them, but they had scales and four feet and were not birds at all."

Father tsked and shook his head.

"Do you know what is wrong with me?" She tumbled into the chair and looked up at him, wrapping her hands around her shoulders.

"Wrong with you? Nothing is precisely wrong with you." Father turned aside and stroked his chin, hardly happy.

"I scarcely think there is anything right with me at the moment."

"You are just like your mother." He frowned and rolled his eyes.

"Mother? She heard things, too?"

"I had hoped you would all be spared the problem, as my dear Elizabeth has. But it seems we are not that fortunate, and you must take on the burden." His lips wrinkled into a very unattractive frown.

"What burden? You are making as little sense as the creatures out in the garden." If only she could stomp as the little puck had.

"Come with me, but do not talk. Nothing must be said in the hearing of the staff." He harrumphed as he led her upstairs.

Anne followed, clinging to the stair railing.

Father opened the door to Mama's room which had been essentially untouched and unused since her death. Was it possible that it still smelled like her? Probably not, but somehow it still did. Maybe just being amidst the pink and yellow rose-covered drapes and bed linens that Mama had chosen made her feel very close.

He shuffled to a dainty mahogany bookcase standing beside the fireplace, laden with many volumes, and pulled out a book—a large, heavy one, bound in blue leather with gold lettering.

"Here. All that you need to know is here. You will find Kellynch among the estates named between those covers. I have been assured it is an honor to be so listed, though it involves considerable effort and no distinction. My father said it was more drudgery and expense than anything else. We are fortunate that all that nonsense has been dormant for decades and nothing has been demanded from us. It is my hope it will stay that way for quite some time."

"I do not understand what you are talking about. How am I to make any sense of this when you speak in riddles?" She clutched one of the slender mahogany bedposts with one hand and held the book close to her chest with the other, squeezing her eyes shut. Father did not like tears, but now it might actually be a reasonable course of action.

He propelled her toward the overstuffed chair near the window. "Read the book. It will answer all your questions." He strode out and shut the door–loud and final—behind him.

Anne fell into the chair's warm, pink and yellow striped embrace and stared at the heavy tome in her lap. She brushed away some lingering dust and cobwebs, but it did not change the title.

The Annals of the Blue Order: Its Tenets, Treaties and Laws with a Complete Listing of All Lands and Dragons Related Thereto

What kind of a joke was he playing at?

July 1809

Late in the day, Anne carried the heavy tome to her room and requested a dinner tray be sent up. That was probably a mistake. Who could eat under the weight of such revelations? She read by candlelight, long into the night.

The next morning, the cool orange rays of dawn woke her, stiff and sore, still curled in her overstuffed burgundy arm chair near the windows. She unfurled. Oh, her neck and back! Her bed, only two steps away, would have been a far more reasonable place to sleep. Was it mocking her, still made up with its rose and green floral counterpane and bed curtains that matched the soft green of her walls?

She rubbed her eyes, stretching protesting legs and rubbing her cold feet against the smooth wooden floor. What strange dreams! At least that dreadful headache was gone. Perhaps now she could start making sense of the world. She pushed off the small round table in front of her chair to stand, her hand landing on a thick, blue, leather-bound book.

Oh, no.

The book—it had not been a dream. The tome she dreamt she read—it was real.

No, no, no!

She landed in the chair with a thump, chair legs screeching on the floorboards, and pulled the volume toward her. It fell open on her lap to the center of the book where woodcuts of frightening creatures were organized into categories and types.

Dragons.

So very many dragons. All supposedly living right beneath her nose.

It sounded like nonsense of the very worst form. But according to the book, dragons were real. And according to Father, the book was an accurate reference to all she was currently experiencing. Had anyone else told her such a thing, she would have declared it a joke at her expense and forgotten about it. But Father? No, his sense of propriety left no room for a sense of humor.

She clutched the sides of her head, rocking.

What did one do with such information? How did one entirely transform one's beliefs about ... nearly everything? To accept that there were dragons in the world and had been for quite some time? Moreover, they had been at war with men, at least until Uther Pendragon struck a peace treaty with them. Then there were the Pendragon Accords. Those formed the Blue Order, a secret organization of those who could hear dragons—for not all could—purposed to maintain the peace between men and dragons (as well as among dragons, but that was another matter altogether.)

Yes, that was certainly sensible and believable.

That only a small minority of people could hear dragon voices—something to do with preternatural hearing that did not really make sense—only made things more complicated and isolating. Worse still, the rest of the world was susceptible to something called a "persuasive voice" that dragons could use to make men believe the dragons were other creatures, or possibly not even there at all.

How did that even make sense? She swallowed back the bile that collected—again—at the back of her throat.

Naturally, The Pendragon Accords regulated just how this "voice" could be legally used and assured that it would prosecute for illegal usage. Naturally.

She shook her head. Perhaps if she shook it hard enough, these ridiculous notions would fall out and the world would make sense again.

This was all stuff and nonsense. She dropped the book on the table and sprang to her feet, nearly knocking off the dinner tray from last night. It had to be. Dragons were nothing but fairy stories for children and frivolous paintings of old. It was not possible for any of it to be true. They could not be hiding in plain sight, and they could not be prevalent in the whole of England.

She needed to move, to break free of these preposterous tales. She paced three circuits around the room and came to a stop at her little oak table where the ludicrous book stared up at her.

If it was all so nonsensical, why would Father direct her to that volume, and why would it have been in Mother's room? Why was he not surprised—or even at all critical of any of her symptoms? His daughter was destined for Bedlam, and he was unconcerned? As much attention as he paid to appearances, one would think the whole affair would send him into extreme agitation.

But he was calm. Frighteningly calm.

She reached for a crust of bread left from dinner and gnawed at it along with a few bits of cheese. Her stomach did not immediately turn arsey-varsey. She swallowed a few gulps of cold tea. Oh, that helped.

Wait, what was that? A little pink ribbon poked out near the end of the book. Could Mama have marked a page? She opened the tome at the ribbon and traced the page with her finger.

Induction into the Order

In so far as the Blue Order exists to protect the peace between mankind and dragonkind, all those who hear dragons must be subject to the Order, either by membership in the Order or under the protective custody of the Order.

Blue Order members must constantly be alert for individuals who may have come into their hearing, especially within their own families. Upon the discovery of a new dragon hearer, the discovering member is responsible for bringing the new hearer to the attention of the Order. Failure to do so is a criminal offense of the first order and will be prosecuted as such.

Officers of the Order, Keepers, Honored Friends and Recognized Friends of the Order may sponsor new members into Order. The sponsoring member...

Wait ... what? Must be subject to the Order...failure a criminal offense of the first order? She swallowed hard as her hand shook while turning the page. A yellowed scrap of paper no larger than her palm written with a very peculiar shade of blue ink stared up at her.

Blue Order

Certificate of Membership
Elizabeth Anne Stevenson
Is duly admitted to all pursuant rights, privileges, and responsibilities of
The Blue Order
Signet number 23091770

This 23rd day of September 1770
Capital Office, London England

A series of official looking signatures scrawled across the bottom of the page. Mama had really been a part of all this. It was real? Mama had been talking to dragons that day in the garden all the while Lady Russell thought it just a silly game?

Anne picked up the certificate and studied it. Incontrovertible proof. This was part of Anne's legacy and her future.

Signet number? Mama had a signet that she kept on her chatelaine, the one Elizabeth wore now. But Elizabeth did not wear the signet ... Anne jumped up and ran to Mama's room. Thankfully the corridors were empty, so she did not have to explain her mad dash.

She flung Mama's door open and pelted to the imposing inlaid oak chest of drawers in the adjacent dressing room. Panting, she jerked the top drawer open. No jewelry box. The second drawer stuck. She braced her feet against the bottom of the chest of drawers and yanked with both hands. Wood squealed against wood—was that a protest or a warning? Inch by inch, the drawer gave way.

There! The ebony and onyx inlaid jewelry box! Her hands shook too hard to remove the box, so she lifted the lid. Tears burned her eyes. Elizabeth had long since taken the pieces Mama had left to her, so had Mary. Sentimental as it was, Anne chose to leave hers in Mama's jewelry box until she finally left home. Yes, it was silly, but it felt right.

She ran her fingertips over Mama's pearls and the cameo she had so loved. A triple strand of coral beads... so many memories. There in the corner—Anne wrapped two fingers around a cold, hard, brass knob. Heavy, with a loop at the top to hang off a chain—a piece not specifically left to any of her daughters.

Dare she look at it?

No, not until there was sufficient light.

Slow, steady steps, silent steps from stocking feet carried her to the window in Mama's bedchamber. The striped chair's warm embrace beckoned, and she answered. Sunbeams caressed and warmed her though her hands remained cold. Holding her breath and biting her lip, she turned the signet seal side up.

A red-flecked, green stone, carved with a dragon that matched the frontispiece of the book she had been reading.

And tiny, precise numbers: 23091770.

She fell back into the chair. Exactly what the certificate had described.

It was real. It was all real.

She pressed the signet to her chest and fought to breathe. The book described the penalties to be enacted upon those who violated the edicts of the Order. These Blue Order people, whoever they were, were very serious about their rules.

Heavens! She heard dragons now. She would have to be presented to the Order! Did Father know?

Even if he did, all things considered, it would be up to her to ensure that it happened. Oh, merciful heavens!

6
Chapter

THE NEXT DAY, Anne waited until Father had finished his breakfast and retreated into his study. Book in hand, heart thundering, she knocked and waited ten long breaths for him to open the door to her.

"Anne? Why are you disturbing me? I have business to attend." He blocked the doorway, the sandalwood scent of his shaving oil filling the space between them.

"This is very important, I am sure." She gazed into his eyes, not giving way.

He stepped aside and allowed her inside, grumbling. "What can you have that could be as important—"

"It is in regards to the Blue Order." She must remain true to her purpose. Any show of weakness ...

He sneered and shut the door behind him. "A band of self-important tyrants and thieves. What from them can be so important?"

Following the ivory stripe on the plush carpet, she stopped at his imposing desk. Several magazines, open to fashion plates illustrating new cuts of men's coats, took up much of the desktop. She sidled around the dark gold, leather-covered wingchair in front of the desk and carefully moved the magazines aside. Laying the book on the desk, she opened it to the pages Mama had marked.

"These regulations seem very important." Why could she not look at his face now, but only at the wall over his shoulder and the painting of Kellynch estate that hung there?

"What are they to me?"

That blue in the curtains, on the carpet, covering the armchairs near the fireplace, it was familiar—the same color as the book binding! Even this room conspired to convince her of her new reality! "It is your responsibility to present dragon-hearing members of your family to the Order. It must be done as soon as might be arranged after the discovery of the new hearer." She pointed out the lines.

"And I believe the same tome also says that girls typically come into their hearing between fifteen and eighteen. You are twenty-two, four years too late for such falderal."

"But, sir, the penalties listed here are quite serious. You do not wish to risk—"

"And what are they going to do to a baronet?"

"Among other things, your name will be read at a Conclave Meeting on a 'List of Dishonor' and you will be shunned by all honorable Dragon Keepers."

"What is their opinion to me?"

"Have you recently looked at the list of Dragon

Estates? So many of the peers are on that list!" Anne pointed to the names. "Do you not care that you will be put out of good company—"

Father snatched the book and stared at the page, his expression darkening as he scanned down. "Ridiculous. None of these people take this dragon business seriously enough to—"

"Do you truly wish to take such an extreme risk, put the name and reputation of the family in jeopardy?"

His complexion turned nearly puce. He would not approve of that color if he could see it. "I have already told Elizabeth that a trip to London while the Dalrymples are not in residence would not happen. How would it look if I were to change my mind for you? No, it cannot be done. I will not travel to London—"

How could he put the family in such danger? He was nothing like the proper Dragon Keeper described in the *Annals*. "London is not the only option." She held her breath. No matter how much she disliked the alternative, she had to present it.

"The Order offices are in London."

"Regional offices exist all over England. Potential members can be presented at any of those offices. The nearest one, the one over Dorset and Somerset, is in Bath. See here." Anne opened the book again and pointed.

"Bath. Bath. Bath." He turned away and paced the length of his study, touching the shelves and cabinets bearing his favorite possessions as he went. "That is an interesting notion."

"It is only a six-hour journey from home, not nearly so much as to London."

"And the company there—"

"Would certainly benefit from the presence of a baronet." Anne winced. Sounding like Elizabeth hurt, but desperation demanded extreme action.

"Yes, of course. We would be appreciated there." He nodded slowly. "That is an interesting notion indeed."

"You could accomplish your duty to the Order, provide Bath with some excellent society, and permit Elizabeth to mingle in good company as she desires, all at very little inconvenience to—"

He flipped his hand toward her.

She bit her lip and waited three more lengths of the long room.

He turned at the fireplace and strode briskly toward her. "We are for Bath. But make no mention of any of these unpleasantries to your sisters; they do not need to be troubled by such things."

"And you will present me to the Order?"

He grumbled something that sounded vaguely affirmative. "I will set Shepherd to arranging a lease."

"Shall I begin preparations?"

"Do consult Elizabeth. She will surely have some opinions."

Yes, she would; she always did. As long as they ended up in Bath, Elizabeth's opinions could be accommodated. But would she be able to adjust one more set of demands, those of the Blue Order, as easily? And how was she to manage not resenting one more authority trying to exert its rule on her life?

"When do you think we might—"

"I expect it should take a week or so to make all the arrangements. You might safely plan a departure then."

A week, she had a week, only a week. To prepare to leave Kellynch; to avoid Lady Russell and her nosy questions; and to refuse Charles Musgrove.

The drive to Bath only took the expected six hours, but the circuit around the principal streets of Bath that Father insisted the driver make before arriving at Camden Place added another hour and a half to the journey. All in Bath must know the Elliots had arrived and see them traveling as befit a baronet's family. Whatever that might mean.

The luggage wagon had arrived in the mews of the first-rate townhouse at the corner of the street before them. The houses toward the middle were grander, Mary had observed; but were not available to let for only a month's stay, Father was quick to inform her. Far be it from him to take a house even slightly less than the best available.

Father, Mary, and Elizabeth hurried inside to investigate the wonders of their new abode while Anne rode on to the mews behind the house to supervise the unloading—what remained of it to be done. The driver and the stable boy who rode the rugged vehicle with him had hurried to get the job done as soon as they arrived. Possibly to avoid dealing with Father and Elizabeth any more than necessary.

After the empty cart pulled out of the mews, Anne wandered to the front of the house, shaking out the skirts of her drab traveling gown. The cobblestones made walking difficult even in her sturdy half-boots; the paths and roads near Kellynch had no such uncomfortable paving. And the way was steep. Was everything in Bath uphill? It had seemed that way when she had been to school here.

Street sounds assailed her. How noisy it was, wheels and hooves clattering against the stone streets. And people's voices—how they echoed here. Would she ever grow accustomed to the weight of all those sounds? Probably not, it was one of the things she had disliked about the city.

A cool breeze off the river blew away a bit of the mid-day heat and seemed to dampen a little of the clamor. It would be interesting living next to a river like the Avon. Her school had been quite some distance from it. The cool water smell alone was so very different to the Kellynch countryside. Did any dragons live in those waters? She rubbed her upper arms with her palms.

Their townhouse stood on the street corner, facing the river. She had not taken the time to really look at it when the rest had debarked. Tall—four rows of windows faced the street—and faced with yellow-orange Bath stone ubiquitous to the city, it seemed compact compared to the manor, a much better fit for a family party of just four than the sprawling corridors of Kellynch. Other townhouses, nearly identical, lined both sides of the street. No doubt, losing the distinction of a unique home set apart from others like Kellynch manor was would be a difficult privation for Father to bear.

Neat ironwork trimmed the front, black as the front door which bore a rather plain brass knocker. If they would be living there more than a month, Father would insist on having that changed.

"Miss Elliot? Miss Anne Elliot?"

That voice, it seemed familiar. Anne turned.

A slim young woman in a dark green walking dress, with a long, regular face under a wide straw hat, peered at her.

Could it be? "Miss Hamilton? I mean, Mrs. Smith?"

"Indeed! How good to see you, Miss Elliot. I had no idea you would be in Bath." She smiled broadly and dipped in a short curtsy.

"We have only just arrived today, just within the hour really."

"Then I really have come at a fortuitous time! Will you be in residence long? My husband and I are living here now, in Pulteney Street. What a goose I am, you already know that since you direct your letters to me there." Mrs. Smith chuckled, her hazel eyes sparkling even as they had during their school days.

"We are to stay a month, I think."

"Pray, may I call upon you? Once you are settled in, of course." There was something unusual about Mrs. Smith. Was it the tenor of her voice or perhaps the way she cocked her head when she listened? Something had changed.

"I would like that very much, indeed. I do not know that I have any other acquaintances in Bath."

"That is a shame. I know my acquaintance may not be as fine as your father would desire, but I would be happy to arrange for introductions for you, if you wish."

She was right; Father would not approve. "I should be happy to meet any friends of yours."

"You have not changed at all from our school days! I am so happy you are here." What had caught the light there, at Mrs. Smith's waist? A chatelaine holding a signet … just like Mama's! "Pray forgive me, I am expected back at home. I must go. But I promise to call as soon as I am able."

Anne pulled her eyes away from the signet. "I will inform the butler that you are expected and are to be shown in when you come."

"You are too gracious." Mrs. Smith curtsied and hurried uphill.

Everything in Bath was uphill.

Five days later, Anne gripped the iron banister as she strode down the wide marble staircase with the perfect posture and grace Elizabeth insisted was appropriate for a lady in Bath, muttering under her breath about the inconstancies of men—Father in particular. He was to have taken her to the Order yesterday, then today, then tomorrow.

Now it was sometime next week. Possibly. He did not know. Possibly.

He had parties and dinners, calls to pay, calls to wait upon being paid. Always something more important than what was truly important. Or at least what was important to her.

His preferences would always prevail. Always. What would it be like to be able to make decisions for herself and make the world subject to those?

The butler waited for her at the foot of the stairs, a silver tray with a calling card held out for her. Tall, somber and impeccably dressed. Exactly the sort of man Father would favor for the job. "Miss, is this the woman who you requested be shown in if she called?"

Anne picked up the card. "Yes, show her to the parlor." He should have already done that, but Father had probably given some sort of contradicting order. At least she had not been turned away.

The butler bowed and turned toward the front door while Anne instructed a maid to bring refreshments to the parlor.

Anne's slippers skimmed along the black and white marble tile as she entered the compact parlor and chose a seat near the gold-draped windows. The parlor faced the diminutive garden in the mews, a far more pleasant and quieter view than looking out onto the busy street corner. The white and gold paper hangings on the walls mimicked swooping taffeta drapes—rather overwhelming for a relatively small room. Ivory and gold wood chairs and tables, and settee with deep gold upholstery helped lighten the space just a little. Though the open windows brought in a breeze, the garden flowers had little perfume and none to lend to the stuffy parlor.

"Mrs. Smith to see Miss Anne Elliot," the butler announced from the doorway.

Mrs. Smith, slim and neat in a brown and red trimmed walking dress, clutched her reticule in both hands. The sunlight caught the chains of her chatelaine—the signet was still there.

"I am so glad you are come. Do sit down." Anne dismissed the butler with a nod.

"I have not been to any house on Camden Place before. It is quite lovely." Mrs. Smith sat on the white and gold painted settee nearest Anne.

"My father finds it tolerable. Elizabeth is disappointed it is not grander."

"They have not changed either, I suppose?" Her voice was so sweet and thoughtful, just as it had been in school.

"No. I am not sure people ever do. But enough of that. Tell me of your new life as Mrs. Smith."

"What is there to tell that has not been in my letters? You know everything already—I think I must bore you with all the drivel of daily life in those missives." She laughed a note of self-deprecation. "Through those you know my husband, our household, even the name by which the housekeeper calls the scullery-maid when she thinks I am not listening. Oh, but wait, there is one new thing I think you will find of particular interest. My husband has recently joined in a new business venture. I realize such things are probably not of great interest to you, but I believe his partner is related to your family. Mr. William Elliot?"

Anne's eyes grew a little wider. "I am all agog. I had no idea that you would know him. He is our cousin and heir presumptive to Kellynch. I have not the pleasure of an acquaintance with him, not yet. But he is to come visit us at Kellynch at the end of the summer. What can you tell me of him?"

"He is a well-looking man, with a good education and proper opinions."

"You approve of him?"

"I do not believe I have ever thought of him in a way to approve or disapprove. It is not my place, though I am told that he is excellent company."

He did not sound like a man equipped to help her current circumstance. Anne sighed. Usually she was better at concealing her disappointment.

"You do not seem like yourself, my friend. Would it be untoward of me to ask what is wrong?"

Dare she? Anne stood and walked to the window, her back to Mrs. Smith. But what other choice was there. "I am in a difficult situation, and I do not know where to turn."

"You think there is something I might help you with? You know I am willing to do what I can."

Anne pulled at the gold chain from under her fichu and freed Mama's signet from its folds. Her fingers trembled as blood roared in her ears. Sometimes one just had to take a chance and trust her heart. "What do you know of this?" She held out the signet, still around her neck.

Mrs. Smith blanched, and her hand went to her own matching piece. "Where did you get that?"

"It was my mother's—"

"You should not have it. It should have been returned when she passed." Mrs. Smith seemed ready to snatch it out of her hands.

"I believe it is right for me to have it. I know. I am … a part of her secrets now."

"When? How?"

Anne briefly related her experiences with Beebalm and Shelby and Father's reactions.

Mrs. Smith pursed her lips and blinked thoughtfully. "Then, you are a member now?"

"That is the problem. I am not, and it seems Father is unwilling to do what is necessary to see that I am presented to the Order." Anne returned to her chair near the windows.

Mrs. Smith gasped. "This is very serious. Have you been prepared to be presented?"

"No. Father wants nothing to do with any of it."

"You have met the estate dragon at least, no?"

"No. Nothing." Estate dragon? She clutched the edge of her seat.

Of course, that made sense; Kellynch was listed as

a dragon estate. That meant there had to be a dragon—a large one. But where was its lair? Did Father even know? He said he had nothing to do with such disagreeable things.

Mrs. Smith pressed her hands to her cheeks. "I do not presume to judge one of your father's station, but this is very serious indeed."

"That is what I understand as well. I do not know what to do. Father cannot be prevailed upon to do what I think is his duty. Who can I even turn to?"

Mrs. Smith wrung her hands. "We are not Dragon Keepers, nor do we even have a Dragon Friend, so I hardly know what to tell you. But you are right; this is a grave matter."

"I have consulted every book at my disposal, and I do not know what to do." Would it be wrong to add that the feeling of not knowing was a very strange and threatening one, indeed?

"You must be recognized by the Order. That cannot happen too soon." Mrs. Smith chewed her knuckle. "I can only think of one thing, and I am not sure it is a very good idea at all."

"Pray tell me. Even a bad idea is welcome at this point."

She fingered her signet, staring at it as though answers might be written there. "Though it is strongly frowned upon by the Order for such an insignificant member to act in such an important capacity, I can take you to the offices and present you for membership myself."

"But if it is against the rules—"

"Technically, I should tell one of them that you now hear and allow them to approach you. But that would only lengthen the process and perhaps make things more complicated. If you are only to be in Bath for a month, it is possible you could leave before the Order even contacts you. I believe the issue of you remaining unconnected to the Order any longer than necessary is serious enough that they will be tolerant of the violation."

"I should not allow you to risk yourself because of my Father's intractability."

"Members of the Order have sworn to hold the preservation of the Pendragon Treaty and Accords above their personal comfort and even their safety. I am quite certain this is what must be done. Have you studied the Treaty and the Accords?"

"As much as I can."

"Good, that will help. You will be tested on your knowledge of them, in detail, particularly because you are the eldest hearing child and likely to become the next Keeper. Above all else, you must know the Treaty and the Accords—not the obscure bits that are only recorded in the Order archives, but the main parts that are printed and available in the home of every Order member."

"While I have had no tutor, I have been applying myself to their study a great deal recently." Anne shrugged slightly.

"You were always very clever at school. If I could pass their examination, I am sure you will be able to as well. We should do it as soon as possible."

"Father has promised he would take me to the Order on Monday next week. If he does not, then perhaps, the next day?" That would give her five more days to study.

"I hesitate to wait even that long, but yes, you are right. It would be best to give him the opportunity to present you properly first."

"I will send you word on Monday, then." And study like she never had in the meantime.

7
Chapter

ON TUESDAY MORNING, Anne slipped from the house with no one but the footman and housekeeper the wiser. No one else was awake at the ridiculous hour of nine o'clock—Father and Elizabeth preferred keeping town hours when they were in town, even if that town was not London. Birds cawed and twittered from the rooftops as if to scold the lay-a-beds.

In half an hour she was to meet Mrs. Smith on Pulteney Bridge. From there, they would walk to the Pump Room—if only they were going for the water! But no, just across the walk from the Pump Room, in an ordinary four-story building with a blue door, her fate awaited.

The cool morning air tasted of the river and an unusual mineral flavor that was, she was told, unique to Bath—something about the baths there. It seemed very pronounced today as she trod the uphill roads toward Pulteney Bridge. She rubbed her shoulders over her spencer. The red-brown linen that matched her roller-print walking dress should have been sufficient protection against the morning chill. But when the chill came from within, warmth proved elusive.

Had she been out for any other reason, she would have stopped to admire the bridge's Palladian-style structure. How many bridges were large enough to accommodate shops along both sides? So unique and unlike anything near Kellynch. Hopefully, she would be able to right that oversight on another day.

Mrs. Smith approached, blue skirts swishing with each brisk step. Was that the same blue as the binding on the volume containing the Pendragon Treaty and Accords? Yes, it seemed so.

Odd, neither Anne nor her sisters had any blue gowns. Father had made it clear that he disliked his daughters in that color. Did that have something to do with the Order?

"Are you ready?" Mrs. Smith touched her arm.

"I do not think I could ever feel ready for such a moment though I have been studying every moment I could snatch away from Father and Elizabeth's demanding social calendar."

"Good, good." She slipped her arm in Anne's. "Then all will be well, I am sure of it. Let us go then and be bold. The Order approves of boldness in its members." They set off down High Street toward Bath Abbey, dodging peddlers' carts and tradesmen's wagons on the street.

"Even in women? The Order approves of boldness in them as well?" Anne whispered.

"Yes, they do. It is to do with the—" she leaned close to Anne's ear and barely said, "—dragons," and returned to speak as before. "They are different to men and prefer unfeigned candor and assurance in all with whom they deal."

"I had no idea."

"I am told it is because they are predators and rather that their warm-blooded companions do not behave like prey. Many ladies I know are uncomfortable with it, and some even avoid Order events because of it. But others, I am told, find it pleasing. I do not think I am that sort, though. There are even Ladies among the officers of the Order and Keepers."

Women in positions of responsibility, alongside men?

"I am sure you will not have to worry about such things, though. I do not believe that any are forced into such responsibilities." She patted Anne's arm. "All you need to focus on is managing today."

Yes, that was good advice. The rest of these heady, terrifying—and possibly delightful—thoughts could wait to be sorted out. Focus on today.

"There it is, you see."

Anne followed Mrs. Smith's chin point to a blue door in the yellow-orange Bath stone building adjacent to the Pump Room. Four stories tall, with cloudy windows and little decoration, the door color was the only reason anyone might make note of it. Odd that no signage should announce an edifice so important. But it did make sense. Dragons were a secret, after all.

An unusual number of birds, large and small, perched on the edge of the roof. She squinted and stared—some of those had long serpentine tails! A guard ready to persuade passers-by that there was nothing unusual to see?

Her heartbeat quickened from slightly anxious to

nearly frantic as they stepped up to the door. Perhaps Mrs. Smith's did, too. Her arm trembled in Anne's. A brass dragon head holding the doorknocker in its jaws looked down on them.

Mrs. Smith looked at Anne, and they nodded. Mrs. Smith rapped the knocker.

A huge man in blue livery—the same distinct blue as the door—opened the door just a fraction, filling the space with his broad frame. "Your business here?"

Mrs. Smith held out her chatelaine. "I have business with the Regional Undersecretary."

"You have an appointment?"

"No, it is urgent. My friend, she has become conversant with ... Pendragon ... and is in need of a further acquaintance."

He examined her signet more closely. "You do not have the rank to sponsor a new member. How could you have brought her uninvited and unannounced?"

Mrs. Smith stammered useless sounds.

"I insisted, sir." Anne held out her mother's signet.

He snatched it from her hand peering closely at it. "This number—it is not yours. How did you come by it?"

"It was my mother's—"

He grabbed a brass watch fob from his waist and put it to his lips, producing a shrill, painful whistle. Three large birds—no not birds, the back half of their bodies were like snakes. What had the bestiaries called them? Cockatrix, cockatrice, something like that, maybe?—swooped down, landing beside them with spread wings as though to contain them.

The largest one in the center, mottled brown with a glistening black beak that looked as sharp as barber's razor and wings that spanned at least as wide as she was tall, squawked at her. "I am Wincombe. I have led the guard on this office for thirty-five years. If you can hear me, tell the butler exactly what I have told you. You—" he pointed his wing at Mrs. Smith, "remain silent."

"The one in the center says, 'I am Wincombe and I have led the guard on this office for thirty-five years. If you can hear me, tell the butler exactly what I have told you.'" Anne stammered so fast the words barely made sense.

The butler looked at Wincombe who squawked and propelled Anne and Mrs. Smith through the front doors into a dark entryway, lit by a sliver of light from a cloudy glass transom window above the door. The vestibule boasted closed doors on three walls and no visible decoration. The butler shut the door and locked it with a heavy bolt. The three cockatrice held Anne and Mrs. Smith in a tight circle with outspread wings, hissing and snapping if they twitched.

"Do not move. Your guard will not be tolerant." The butler all but ran to the farthest door and disappeared through it.

"Do not fear, it will be well," Mrs. Smith whispered. "If we obey and do as we are asked, no harm will come to us."

"Is this what you meant by the Order's understanding?"

"We are being quite understanding and lenient, young woman," Wincombe snapped, and the others cawed in agreement. "But do not test our patience."

She had already guessed that much. Those beaks were fit to shred meat, and their talons like daggers. Not creatures to be dealt with lightly.

"What is all this about!" A rather ordinary-looking man in a dark tail coat and trousers, notable only for his complete baldness and pronounced scars on the left side of his head, burst in. His voice, though, it was as shrill as the cockatrice's squawk.

"She—" the butler pointed, "has brought a non-member here. And she—" he pointed at Anne, "brings a signet not her own to present to us."

"It was my mother's."

"Where is your mother?" the scar-headed man demanded.

"She is dead. I am heir to her legacy."

"Heir, you say? Who was she?"

"Lady Elliot of Kellynch Hall."

Two of the cockatrice gasped and rustled their wings.

"Kellynch Hall? That would make you Miss Elizabeth—"

"No, her second daughter, Anne Elliot."

"Well, that explains a great deal. Indeed, it does." The scar-faced man stroked his chin with his fist. "I will escort them from here, Captain Wincombe. Well done. You and your guards may go."

Captain? The creature had a rank like a soldier?

He waved the cockatrice away. "Pray come with me, ladies. I am Peter Wynn, Regional Undersecretary for Dorsetshire and Somersetshire." He gestured for them to walk with him.

Anne took Mrs. Smith's arm. The poor dear was pale and a little glassy-eyed, not without good reason. In all likelihood, Anne was, too. Who could have anticipated such a reception?

Mr. Wynn opened the door at the end of the vestibule and ushered them through it.

Merciful heavens! The wide, tall corridor, lit by cloudy glass windows that reflected off many mirrors, and candles throughout, bustled with men, women, and dragons—from tiny fairy dragons to large snake-type creatures to medieval dragons—drakes, they were called?—easily as large as a man. And none of them acted as though it were anything unusual.

The smell, though! Was that the dragon? It had a vaguely barnyard feel to it, but nothing like horses or cows or sheep—something rather musky and a bit acrid, entirely unique. Unlike anything she had ever known, but not necessarily unpleasant.

The crowd made way for them, a few—human and dragon—gawking as they walked past toward a wide staircase, far wider than any she had ever seen in a building this size. Portraits of somber-faced men, women and dragons lined the white plastered walls over the chair rails and up the marble stairs. Tiny placards she could not read while walking in such haste bore what were probably names and ranks and dates. They left the stairs at the second floor and turned right on a polished wood floor, scuffed a mite in the center with something that resembled claw marks. Again, white walls—was that to make the best use of light?—lined the corridor, punctuated by many closed, carved doors, with transom lights above.

The first door—again far wider than would normally be expected—bore a brass plate: *Regional Undersecretary of Dorsetshire and Somersetshire. Mr. Peter Wynn.* It would have been nice if it told her more than she already knew, but that would have been asking a great deal.

He pushed the door open, herded them inside, and directed them to a pair of stern wooden chairs in front of an imposing, marble-topped desk. A cloudy glass window lit the room from the far side with no curtains to soften the white walls. The smells of paper, old books, and that same peculiar, musky-acrid odor hung in the air. A weathered burgundy-brown carpet took up much of the floor space, but it looked ragged, as though roughed by claws. Bookcases and cabinets lined the walls adjacent to the window. Loose papers and journals occupied nearly every flat surface. Between the bookcase and corner, on the same wall as the door, an opening, without a door and too short for Anne to enter without stooping, led off into darkness.

He sat behind the desk, also cluttered with what appeared to be various works in progress, and pointed at Mrs. Smith. "Who are you, and what is your role in all this?"

"I am Mrs. Smith, a friend of Miss Elliot. She has just come into her hearing."

He pulled open a drawer, not looking at them. "And you are the daughter of Sir Walter Elliot of Kellynch Hall?"

"I am."

"Why is your father not presenting you?"

"He had other pressing social engagements and could not spare the time." Engagements like presenting himself at the Pump Rooms to be seen, attending concerts and suppers and card parties which required him to sleep very late the next morning.

"So, you, Mrs. Smith, a member without status or dragon connections, have brought her in his stead? With his acknowledgement and permission, I assume?" He pulled out a thick folio and laid it on his desk.

"He is not aware, no." Anne wrung her hands. "That is on my insistence. I have been impatient to be presented."

"I see." He drummed his fingers on the folio, the thick leather muffling the sound. "I have many more questions for you, but they may not be asked of one not a member of the Order, so I suppose we should address that issue immediately. Have you studied the Pendragon Treaty and Accords?"

"I have."

"Well, at least something has gone right," he muttered under his breath and rang a bell that had been hidden beneath a pile of papers.

A moment later a dragon—was it a drake?—about the size of Shelby came running in through the open doorway in the back corner of the room. Black and red striped, with a ridge running down its spine and very long talons, its bright jet eyes sparkled with intelligence. Around its neck it wore a livery badge on a blue ribbon. Perhaps it was the source of the carpet's demise.

"Jasper, take Mrs. Smith to the parlor and fetch her a cup of tea. We may be at this for some time."

Jasper nodded. "Pray come with me." Her voice was smooth and silky, rather more like a lady's maid than a dragon's. "I will keep you company until your friend is able to join you again."

"Will you be all right?" Mrs. Smith stood.

"I do not think I have much choice. Go and enjoy your tea." Anne forced a smile and a moment later she was alone with Mr. Wynn. "What will happen if I do not pass your test?"

"You will remain our guest here until such time as you do."

"A prisoner?"

"A guest. If you are deemed intractable, then you will be assigned to a custodial care home in Scotland. You might then consider yourself a prisoner."

"I see."

"Has none of this been explained to you?"

She shook her head vigorously.

"Then you should understand that all hearers of Dragons must come under the auspices of the Order, either as willing members, preferably as members who contribute to the good of dragon society, or under the protective custody of the Order, ensuring that no harm comes to dragon society through them. Those are the only options." No one would accuse him of being direct.

"As I much prefer the first alternative, let us seek that path." Boldness, Mrs. Smith said boldness was appreciated.

"Very good. Then let us begin." He tapped his desk and squared his shoulders.

He peppered her with questions, demands to recite certain passages from memory, and several scenarios in which she was to analyze the application of the treaty. With no way to see the sun, no clock visible in the room, all sense of time dissolved into his endless interrogation.

"It seems, that is to say I think that the actions of the wild wyrm, by hunting on the estate without permission of the estate dragon constitute a trespass, but not one meriting capital punishment. Two warnings by the estate dragon are required before the wyrm can be legally eaten." Anne forced herself to hold her weary shoulders up and look toward Mr. Wynn, but over his shoulder, not in his eyes. Had she really just said such a thing and expected to be taken seriously? Surely this must be the antechamber of Bedlam.

He huffed and frowned and chewed his lips, then stood and paced three times around the room.

Merciful heavens, now what?

"Well, Miss Elliot, while your understandings are imperfect and in need of refinement, they are sufficient to admit you into the Order. Congratulations."

All strength drained from her joints, and she fell back into the hard, wooden chair. "I am accepted, then?"

"Yes. However—"

She hated that word.

"That is not the end to the matter. Your case is complicated." He returned to his chair and pulled a stack of papers out of the folio and scanned them.

"I trust you will explain what that means."

"I suppose you have not met your estate dragon?"

"No, I have not, nor—since I expect you will also ask—have I had any actual training in any aspect of what it means to be a Dragon Keeper." Anne clenched her hands hard, just in case they might be shaking outwardly as much as she did within. Boldness was entirely overrated.

"That makes this exceedingly complicated." He frowned. "Kellynch is far from a model dragon estate. Quite the opposite. The dragon, Kellynch, has not been seen at a Conclave or regional meeting in decades. There are unconfirmed rumors he is not just eschewing the meetings, but that he may be hibernating altogether."

"Dragons hibernate?" Is that what Father meant when he called the matters "dormant?"

"Some species do, particularly if they are unhappy

with their Keepers …"

Anne winced. "And you suspect that all might not be well at Kellynch Hall?"

"We do not suspect; we are certain and have been for some time. There has simply not been sufficient agreement on the situation for the Order to intervene. But now you are here, a relatively simple solution presents itself."

"And what might that be?" Why did the image of a virgin offered in sacrifice to an angry dragon keep flashing through her mind?

"The eldest dragon-hearing son usually inherits the estate—"

"Wait, not the eldest son?"

"Not if he does not hear dragons. Generally, though, inheritances go on without our intervention. We only interfere when necessary."

"My father has no sons."

"That has been part of the problem. His heir presumptive, while a member of the Order—let us say he has not been raised to be a Keeper."

"I still do not understand."

"I am afraid with the estate dragon unhappy enough to hibernate—which I assume is the case—the Elliot family has failed as Dragon Keepers and is in danger of being removed from the land altogether."

Anne clutched the arms of the chair. "You cannot do that."

"The land belongs to the dragon, not to your family. Yes, we can."

"Lose the land? It would be the death of my father." What would become of them?

"That is not our problem. Managing the dragon is.

Happily, for you and your family, there is something you can do in all this."

"Me? What can I do?"

"Become an active junior Keeper. Bring the estate under proper regulation and meet Kellynch's needs when he awakens. Fulfill your family's duty to the dragon, and the estate will remain in the Elliot name." Mr. Wynn leaned back, crossed his arms over his chest and shrugged as though it were all simple and obvious.

"How am I to do that? I am a woman."

"That matters not to dragons. As the eldest dragon-hearing child, the Keepership is your role to inherit, Miss Elliot. You will be Keeper to Kellynch."

"How? The estate is entailed away—"

"The simplest solution and the one I strongly—" the word took an ominous edge, "recommend is for you to marry Mr. Elliot. Then you will remain at Kellynch to do your duty to the dragon and the Order, and the legal order of inheritance can be followed without issue."

"I am to be forced to marry a man I have never even met? Forced marriages are illegal."

"Technically, that is correct. Consider it then the most favorable alternative for all those connected to the matter."

"How precisely am I to contrive such an outcome?" Did she even want to? Her stomach churned.

"The Order will encourage him. Marriage is a business arrangement. We will help him to see it is to his advantage. You can certainly see how it would be to yours. All you have to do is show him what a social asset you can be to him, and I am sure it will be easily accomplished. You are not the romantical sort, are you?"

"No, I do not think so."

"Then what is there to object to? The dragon will be happy, the laws of men satisfied, and the needs of the Order will be met. What woman does not want to be well-settled, and in a home like Kellynch Hall? Truly, it is the best possible outcome."

What woman, indeed? But at what cost? She had refused Wentworth, whom she loved, because of Lady Russell's insistence; Charles Musgrove, whom she did not, by her own best judgment. But to save her family, she now had to marry a man of whom she knew nothing?

Was this what it meant to be part of the Blue Order?

8
Chapter

Lyme, July 1809

WENTWORTH CRADLED LACONIA in the crook of his arm as he strode down Lyme's cobbled main street among the carts and peddlers and foot traffic. Damned uncomfortable stuff to walk upon. Smooth decking was much better.

The sun was mostly hid by the buildings, leaving the chill salt air, tasting of an incoming storm, to gust through the streets and alleys, accosting the pedestrians as it would. Wentworth pulled Laconia in a bit closer, to keep the wyrmling warm against his waistcoat, under his deep blue wool tailcoat. A few passers-by with coats wrapped tight over their chests glanced at him with raised eyebrows.

"Just a man with a cat, leave us be." Laconia murmured and the would-be gawkers turned aside down a narrow alley that they probably did not really need to traverse.

Wentworth chuckled under his breath. How persuasive Laconia had become. Was it odd to be proud of his little Friend for that? He stroked Laconia's silky fur and scratched beneath his chin, the edge of his forefinger rasping gently along the edge of one prominent fang. It had become a joke among his crew as to whether or not the ship's cat would grow into his fangs.

Though only a few months old now, Laconia had grown considerably since his hatching. Still too small for Wentworth to feel safe letting him walk on the streets, he was the size of a small cat, his tail long enough to wrap most of the way around Wentworth's waist.

Even so, the tatzelwurm had what Wentworth's mother would have called an old soul. Far more mature than some of Wentworth's young sailors and even a midshipman or two, Laconia was serious and focused, two traits rarely or perhaps never before ascribed to a tatzelwurm.

That was what made this whole venture so unlikely to succeed. Who paid attention to ideas from a dragon whose type was believed by most to be nearly as addlepated as fairy dragons? But he had promised Laconia to try, and he was a man who kept his promises, so to the Blue Order office they would go.

"Is that the place?" Laconia pointed with his thumbed paw toward a townhouse with a distinct blue door.

"Could you tell by the door or by the squad of cockatrice perched on the roof?" Wentworth paused—four, no, six of the poised, stately creatures, as still and watchful as gargoyles peered down upon all who passed.

"When one has nearly been prey, one is always aware of the local predators." A little shudder ran down Laconia's spine.

"Well, I assure you, you needn't worry about the Blue Order guard. They are far more concerned about the local men causing problems than about minor dragons. If you look closely you can see they all wear black sashes across their chests. They are in mourning, along with the entire office, for the Captain of their Guard, Commodore Easterly's Friend."

Laconia pushed back hard into Wentworth's arm, purring. Sensitive little creature.

Dramatically smaller than the great central headquarters in London, this local office was nearly indistinguishable from the mundane terraced homes on either side. The offices, housed in a four story, first rate town house—hid in plain sight, rather like the dragons themselves.

He strode to the blue doors, under the watchful eyes of the cockatrice guard, and rapped the brass doorknocker—a drake's head holding a large ring. Holding his breath, he waited. He had sent a note ahead to Easterly. Hopefully they would be granted an audience, not be laughed at and turned away at the front door.

A blue-liveried footman, everything somber, serious and formidable, opened the door. "You have business here?"

"Captain Wentworth. I have an appointment with Commodore Easterly." Wentworth lifted his hand to show his signet ring, heavy and clumsy on the small finger of his right hand. He never wore it when he sailed, too much in the way. But on land, it was a necessary convention.

The footman grunted and ushered them into a stark white vestibule with polished limestone tiles, sealed off from the rest of the building by a white paneled door bearing an imposing iron lock. A transom window over the door glazed with foggy glass provided the only source of light. Once the front door was closed and locked, the footman selected a large, dragon-headed key from his fob, opened the far door, and beckoned them to follow.

The door opened into an active space. The main hall continued toward the back of the house, just to the left of the grand staircase—except that it was not so grand, rather more ordinary really. A wider than average corridor opened to the left, near the foot of the stairs. Several well-dressed men, a lady, two small drakes wearing livery badges and black bands around their front right legs, and several smaller dragons, whose types he could not quite identify, stopped their activities and turned to glance at them as they entered.

Laconia huddled back into Wentworth's shoulder. This was his first time to meet a large complement of dragons—well, land dragons in any case—at once. Poor creature was understandably nervous.

"Follow me. I will show you to the Commodore's office." The footman guided them down the left-hand corridor, tiled with the same limestone as the vestibule, and dimly lit by sunlight pouring out from transom windows over each of the closed doors in the hall. Mirrors mounted near the ceiling and stark white paint on the walls helped multiply the light, but even so, the effect was a mite cave-like.

The third door on the left bore an engraved brass placard: *Commodore R. Easterly, Regional Liaison to His*

Majesty's Navy. The footman rapped on the plain oak door three times and opened it.

"Wentworth! Yes, come in. I have been expecting you—both of you." Easterly, tall and broad chested, with a shock of prematurely white hair, sauntered toward them, wearing his blue naval uniform, a black band around his right arm. Weary lines creased the side of his eyes. The loss of his Friend had been difficult.

The office was cramped, like one on a ship. Several narrow offices must have been carved out of a larger front room when the Order took this house for its quarters. Dim sunlight filtered through the frosted glass of a single tall window. Charts and maps, scattered across the white walls, some properly framed, others merely tacked to the walls, fought for space with a large hickory bookcase, shelves bowing under the weight of books and navigation equipment. In the center of it all stood an oak desk so large it barely left room for Easterly to sidle around it. Several plain wooden chairs flanked it. Behind and to the right of Easterly's chair stood a dragon perch draped in black crepe.

"Thank you for seeing us. I know it is not a good time. May I present my Friend, Laconia." Wentworth strode in, extending his arm with Laconia on it slightly.

"Pleased to make your acquaintance." Easterly extended his hand to Laconia, fingers curled toward himself.

Laconia sniffed his fingers, his palm. Unsatisfied, Laconia curled himself around to sniff the back of Easterly's hand, his wrist and halfway up his arm. Laconia smelled everything as long and deep as wise men read contracts. How could he understand so much with just his nose?

Finally, Laconia ducked his head under Easterly's hand. He obliged by scratching behind Laconia's ears. A propitious start, indeed.

"Sit, sit." Easterly trundled toward his desk, piled with charts, maps and journals. "So how have you taken to sea life, young Laconia? Does it agree with you?" He gently moved the dragon perch aside, hand lingering briefly on the black crepe, and sat down.

Wentworth sat on the unpadded wooden chair nearest the desk, Laconia perched on his lap.

Laconia licked his thumbed paw. "Quite well, thank you. It is everything my Friend promised it would be."

"The men quite dote on him. They think him quite lucky." Wentworth scratched behind Laconia's ears.

"Is that so? I am not surprised, black ... cats ... especially the many-toed variety are particularly welcome." Easterly leaned back in his chair, arms crossed over his chest—a man waiting to be impressed.

"There is a great deal more than luck involved, sir. I think you know that." Wentworth nudged Laconia. If he was going to speak his mind, now might be his only chance. He probably did not realize how unusual it was for a tatzelwurm, much less a wyrmling, to be given an audience with a man of Easterly's rank.

"Mrrooow. Indeed, he is right. Good fortune requires a great deal of careful intervention." Laconia unwound his tail from Wentworth's waist and sat up very tall and straight, like a young man testing for lieutenant, and stepped on to the desk.

"And what kind of intervention might that be?" Easterly asked.

"Are you aware of how many marine dragons, and bird-type dragons one encounters on the seas?"

Bless the man for keeping a straight face! "No, tell me."

"You sail regularly?" The tip of Laconia's tail flicked, the way it did when he was about to pounce on a mouse.

"Quite regularly. On those voyages, I have seen only a few bird types and fewer marine dragons than I can count on one hand."

"Then you are not a good observer."

"See here young ... Laconia! I did not invite you here to insult me."

"I mean no insult to you. I only make an observation. My Friend can attest that we see many more marine dragons than you describe, sometimes even daily."

"Forgive me, sir, but he is correct." Wentworth stroked the ruffled fur along Laconia's spine. "I did not believe it myself, at first, but Laconia has introduced me to scores of marine wyrms, herds of hippocampi like my brother Croft's friend White—"

"Herds? White is not a rare sort of creature?" Easterly's eyes went wide. Now he was paying attention!

"Hardly, no, sir. They travel in large groups, like horses on land, but they are shy and generally stay away from ships. White is of an unusually friendly disposition."

"I say, that is remarkable."

"That is not all." Wentworth leaned in. "We have met serpent-whales of many shapes and sizes—"

"Wait, sizes? Serpent whales, there are minor serpent-whales?"

"Indeed, curious, and often very friendly, and helpful creatures."

"You have been conversing with them?" Now they had him!

"Regularly. That is what brings us here. I—we—have a proposal." Laconia chirruped, head cocked.

"You have my attention, do go on. Tell me more about your conversations with these sea dragons. What have they told you?" Easterly's voice was level, but he was chomping at the bit for more.

"It is not just what they have told us, but what we have told them." Wentworth permitted the edge of his lips to rise just a mite.

"We have told them about the Pendragon Treaty." Laconia's tail swept across the desk, careful not to disturb the clutter.

"The Treaty? That seems quite forward, even beyond the bounds—"

"Dragons have asked. Many are interested in the Treaty and the protections it offers." Wentworth shrugged. Should it be this much fun to bait the man? Probably not, but it was gratifying to see him distracted from his loss.

"They are? I had no idea ..."

"Many have found themselves harried by various vessels. They would welcome relief from the interference and perhaps even some protection." Laconia purred softly. "Not to mention the territory battles fought with one another ...."

"Many we have spoken to want to know more about the possibilities. The *Laconia* has acquired something of a name on the seas, and dragons seek us out now. Often."

"That did not take long. You have been sailing together only a few months." Easterly stroked his chin.

"That should tell you something, no?" Wentworth said.

"And the men on your ship, what do they say to all these odd experiences?"

"Those who do not hear simply see what Laconia tells them to see."

"You are that persuasive?"

"Mrrooow." Laconia flicked his tail happily. "What is more, these dragons are often ready to share information with us, tell us where good fishing is or storms to avoid."

"We think, perhaps, they might be encouraged to tell us more than that. They might be able to help us find prize ships, even locate the enemy."

"You want them to be spies for us? That is an outlandish idea, even coming from a tatzelwurm." Easterly snorted and waved off the notion, but it was a little half-hearted.

Laconia spring-hopped closer to Easterly, landing in the middle of a map, fur standing on end, growling. "You doubt me. We have followed their information. The most recent prize ship is the result."

Easterly gaped at Wentworth.

"He speaks the truth. I admit, I thought it rubbish when I first heard, but I am convinced it is worth pursuing."

"You are a very young dragon—we are not in the habit of trusting younglings with serious matters."

"You are when it is necessary." Laconia's tail lashed, knocking papers off the desk.

Easterly crossed his arms over his chest, tucked his chin, and frowned, but it seemed a forced expression. "No, I cannot support this notion. Neither of you is a trained diplomat. We cannot risk it, there is too much at stake. We can hardly manage the landed dragons in the Kingdom. There are no less than three significant estates in jeopardy—at least Kellynch is hibernating— or we think he is—and not an imminent danger ..."

Kellynch? Kellynch was a dragon estate? And the dragon was hibernating? How had he not been aware? Had Edward known when he was made curate at Monkford?

"... then there is the possibility of unknown dragon tunnels leading who knows where—"

"You are too late. It has already begun." Laconia bared his fangs just a little. "If we stop speaking to them now there is no telling how they will react to the insult."

"Sir, recall, we are dealing with dragons, not men. Their notion of diplomacy is far different to ours. If you think about it, they opened the discussions, not us. A serpent-whale asked me about the fabled Pendragon Treaty. We had said nothing. But then we realized the potential of what had begun. Consider what it could mean to England to have an alliance with sea dragons."

Easterly scrubbed his face with his hand. "I cannot agree to what amounts to negotiations with foreign powers without the approval of ... perhaps the king himself!"

"We are not nearly at that point! Just give us approval to seek their assistance in finding prize ships and to watch for incursions by the French. We will not count on their assistance, but we can see if it is even feasible. Simply allow us to test the waters."

"And you—" Easterly point to Laconia, almost touching his nose with his fingertip, "You, young wyrmling, you believe you are equal to such a great task?"

Laconia looked over his shoulder at Wentworth. "My Friend trusts me. I owe him everything, and I would not allow him to come to harm."

"Oh, bloody hell! The whole notion is daft as a bag of bugs, but my late Friend regularly had ideas of the sort. And they were nearly all sound." Easterly threw his head back and stared at the ceiling. "For his sake, and to honor his memory, I give you leave to talk to these sea dragons and learn what you can. But promise them nothing from the Order, not yet. Do not commit to anything bigger than you, Wentworth, can deliver yourself. If you make me regret this, it will be the end of your career. Are you willing to risk that?"

Laconia turned to face Wentworth, great gold eyes wide and focused. Tatzelwurms were flighty and unreliable. No person of sense trusted one with anything significant, much less a career.

But Laconia was different. Even so young, he was stable, stalwart, and completely trustworthy. What was more, in just a few short months, he had given Wentworth back a part of his soul that he thought irrevocably lost. How could he not trust Laconia after that?

"I am willing sir. You will not regret this."

9
Chapter

August, 1809

THE NEXT THREE weeks in Bath were ... what was the best word to describe them? Interesting? Memorable? Challenging? Difficult?

After her admission into the Order, Father was invited to attend an official ceremony to mark the occasion. He refused.

Mrs. Smith and her husband attended, having been given a special dispensation to permit them to become her sponsors to the Order, at least temporarily, until such time as her father accepted his responsibility. That would easily be years, or not at all. Thankfully, the Smiths understood and were ready to accept the possibility.

Since they were not Dragon Keepers themselves or even Friends, they could offer her little in the way of actual guidance. But they would not regret their choice. She might not have left school with an under-standing of the classical languages, but she had been taught history, geography, French, and Italian. If she could learn those, she could learn whatever the Blue Order required. Especially considering how accom-modating they were in identifying the books she would need most and arranging for them to be sent to Camden Place.

Father, on the other hand, was not nearly so pleased. A whole trunk full of books that would have to return to Kellynch with them would be highly in-convenient when the luggage cart had been nearly full when they arrived. Elizabeth would have new gowns to take back with them. Surely, all those books were not necessary, were they?

The Undersecretary's call, or rather calls, as it took three before Father was "in" to receive him, were even less appreciated, involving much shouting. Anne could hear the animated discussions quite clearly de-spite being in the ladies' sitting room on the floor above Father's office. So, this was what it meant to enjoy—or perhaps endure—the preternatural hearing Blue Order members had that allowed them to per-ceive sounds that others could not. At least it was only her who could hear what was going on –the servants should not be privy to hearing their master dressed down so very eloquently.

Irresponsible, unscrupulous, vain, lazy, and self-ish—words no one else dared use with Father were spoken—or yelled, with abandon. It was difficult to say that Mr. Wynn was wrong, not when he support-ed each claim with so very much damning evidence. Father did at least agree that Anne would have the role as junior Keeper—whatever that meant—but that he would not have her putting on airs she did not deserve because of it. Naturally. Mr. Wynn did not find the attitude pleasing and ended his call with a final warning to see that the Dragon Keeping on Kellynch improved. It probably fell upon deaf ears, despite the volume at which it was delivered. Mr. Wynn was not admitted to Camden Place after that.

He did, though, send an additional box of books and a handwritten journal written by a junior Keeper on another estate some fifty years ago. On first glance, it appeared to be written in great detail, far more than any of the books she had read offered. While appreciated, it made it difficult not to wonder how much of the practice of Dragon Keeping was accurately recorded in all those published tomes and how much of it was actually passed from one generation to another by word of mouth. All things considered, though, it was quite possible Father had already passed to her everything he knew.

Merciful heavens! At least with the Smiths, she would not be alone.

The drive back to Kellynch passed with Father and Elizabeth remarking upon the social success their visit to Bath had been. Thankfully, they kept each other occupied with recounting their engagements and required nothing of Anne but to nod occasionally as Mary tried hard to insert her own observations into the discourse.

So much needed to be done to undo the years of neglect at Kellynch. Mr. Wynn had strongly suggested that since Kellynch was hibernating, she needed to begin by attending to the minor dragons of the estate and then try to estimate how much longer Kellynch would be sleeping. The former was fairly straightforward, the latter unfortunately was not.

The day they returned and the next, Anne had to supervise unpacking and manage several issues with the servants that Elizabeth simply did not want to bother with. The following day, she rose early. The rest of the family was still keeping town hours; even so, she rushed through her ablutions to be certain she could make her escape.

She headed to the west side of her mother's garden where the fairy dragons often played. The little gossips and snoops, the fairy dragons should be an excellent source of information on the current minor dragons inhabiting Kellynch.

The sun peeked just above the horizon with barely light enough to permit her to walk. The cool, slightly damp morning air embraced her, soothed her. Dew-laden grasses and flowers kissed her muslin skirts, leaving them cold and clinging to her ankles. It probably would have been a good idea to have brought a shawl, but she would just have to make do. If she walked a little faster, she would be warm enough.

Odd. How she had not noticed the border of many-colored snapdragons along the garden's western edge? Mama liked all sorts of flowers as much as she liked little puns. Surely this one had been intentional, given how the fairy dragons frequented the flower bed.

"Pray come out, little ones, I have come to talk to you."

"It is true! It is true!" The voice overhead was high and shrill, like the voice of a songbird, if such a creature could speak.

Anne squinted and scanned the garden. There

above her, three of the tiny creatures hovered, their usually vivid colors muted by the wan morning light.

"You spoke to us! You know our true nature!" Was it the largest one speaking?

"What are we going to do? What are we going to do?" Two smaller ones flew circles over her head.

"Whatever do you mean? You are becoming twitter-pated for nothing." That voice was familiar. Very, very familiar.

Anne's face turned cold. No! That was not possible.

The larger one swooped above Anne's head and toward a large hardwood tree shading a small white wooden gazebo. "She knows nothing of our kind. Nothing of the Blue Order. We are all in grave peril, very grave. She is surely a danger to us."

"Her father is a member of the Order, a lazy disreputable one, but he is. For all his failings, he will not allow harm to come to dragonkind on his estate. Of that I am entirely certain." That familiar voice again, from behind the tree.

"He is no Keeper. Look how he has managed the territory," one of the little ones scolded.

"Simply being lazy and selfish does not make one a danger. I will see to it myself; all will be well." Lady Russell? That voice sounded like Lady Russell! "Her mother was a great friend to dragons. There is no doubt her daughter will be as well. I shall teach her; you need not fear." Lady Russell communed with these creatures, too? Like Mama did?

Was it possible? There was someone sensible who could help her? Something very much like hope rose in her breast. She rushed toward the gazebo to find Lady Russell.

Long stalks and twining vines conspired to slow her, but the foul things would not prevail. She broke through the garden clutter into a small clearing around the tree and gazebo. The fairy dragons dove in and out of the tree branches, wings flapping a little wildly.

Where was Lady Russell?

Anne peeked around the wide tree trunk. A tall, brightly blue bird with an impossibly long neck turned to look at her. What was that? The tail—long and elegant—resembled both a peacock in color and an ostrich in the fluffiness of the feathers. It stood nearly as tall as she. The beak was sharp and curved like a hawk's, and the eyes huge and glittering, with the longest eyelashes imaginable. There were no creatures like that on the estate. Possibly not anywhere.

It turned to her and looked her in the eyes. "Good day, Anne." It spoke in Lady Russell's voice.

Everything turned cold and dark, and the ground rushed up to meet her.

Anne opened her eyes and screamed. Dark, sparkling eyes stared down at her over a long vaguely yellow beak.

"That is hardly a way to greet me. But I suppose you are not well. Did you hurt yourself when you fell?" the enormous bird asked in Lady Russell's voice, turning its head this way and that.

Anne sat up and scrabbled back through the dirt, head and shoulder throbbing where they had struck the ground. "What are you?"

"Whatever do you mean by that? That is no way to speak to your old friend." The creature extended its wings slightly as though perching hands on hips.

"Get away from me! I have never seen you be-fore."

"Of course, you have."

"You sound like Lady Russell, but you are not her. Leave me alone!"

"Of course, I am, just as you have always known me." The voice changed subtly, rasping against her flesh like a whetstone on steel.

Anne cringed and covered her ears. "Stop that!"

"Stop what? I am Lady Russell. Stop looking at me that way. Now get up, and let me take you back to the house. I knew I should have called upon you when you returned from Bath. I had a feeling you were un-well."

"Stop making those sounds that hurt my head. I do not know what they are, but you must stop them." Anne clambered to her feet and stepped back. "I shall not be going anywhere with you. Now tell me what you are."

"I am Lady Russell." That horrid sound continued, and the creature stomped.

Anne spun on her heel and stormed away. Dare she go back to the house? Wherever she went, she had to get away from here and that bird-thing that made her head ache so. Blast it all, the creature was following. "I said leave me alone. Go on! Shoo!"

She picked up her pace, crashing through careful-ly-maintained flower beds, batting at stalks and blossoms as she went.

There, at the far side of Mother's gardens, Father's pride and joy, his conservatory! Yes, she could find refuge within the tall windows and verdant plants. She scurried inside and locked the door behind her. Lungs begging for breath, she fell back against the door, panting. Warm, tranquil air embraced her with the peaceful silence only green and growing things could offer. The scent of fresh soil and quiet, blissful quiet! At last—

Rapping at the window! The creature pecked at the windows.

"Go away! You are not wanted here!" Anne waved the creature off.

"Do show some sense, and let me in. I am Lady Russell." It scratched at the dirt with long talons, throwing a bit of a fit.

That was rather like Lady Russell.

Anne clutched her head against the stabbing pain behind her ears. "I will call the gamekeeper and have him shoot you, you wretched creature, if you do not leave me alone."

The creature stopped and took a step back, its long neck pulling back even further. "What do you see when you look at me?"

"Certainly not Lady Russell."

"Are you sure?"

"Of course, I am." She balled her fists and stomped. "Lady Russell is not a five-foot-tall blue bird with the tail feathers of a peacock."

The yellow-orange beak hung agape, and its eyes grew even wider. "Is that what you see?"

"Of course not, I am simply making that up because I want to vex you." Probably not the right thing to say, but—

"That is a bit of a problem, then." The creature stepped back, hunched, and stood on one foot, tucking the other up into her belly feathers until it all but disappeared. Somehow, she looked as though she were thinking. "Are you certain—"

"Entirely."

The creature sighed, its long dangling head feathers drooping just a bit. "This does complicate matters. But I should not be surprised, you are, indeed, just like your mother. Pray let me inside, and I shall explain everything."

"And you will stop calling yourself Lady Russell?"

"That I cannot do. I am your friend and your mother's friend whom you have known as Lady Russell."

The world around her threatened to spin again. She gulped in several large breaths. "But you are no lady."

"No, I am not. I am a dragon."

"Of course. Naturally, that is absolutely the most sensible explanation for everything!" Nothing she had yet read gave her to expect such a thing. Should she laugh or cry? Both were equally possible right now.

Why were her hands shaking? It was not fear; no, she was not afraid. The blood roaring in her ears, the knots in her belly—that was … anger?

"Do let me in, and I shall tell you everything. I do not like talking to you through this glass." The creature pecked at the window.

It was an odd feeling; one she had never permitted herself to indulge in. Yes, that was it, she was angry. "I do not appreciate any of this … this charade!"

"I can see that, but there is little that can be done about it with me on the other side of this door. Do let me in." It rapped the glass again.

"Only if you agree not to make those horrid, hurtful sounds again."

It cocked its head to and fro. "I suppose you are right. I agree. Now, the door?"

What else was she to do? She opened the conservatory door and ushered the creature in.

It—she?—strolled in with impossibly long steps that were uncomfortably like Lady Russell's movements, and circled Anne, her head bobbing back and forth as she did. "You do not look well, you know."

"I do not feel very well, either."

"Do sit down. There is a bench just over there." The creature gestured with her wing and sauntered toward it, long talons scraping against the slightly sandy stone floor.

What point in arguing? Anne followed and settled herself on the hard, decidedly lopsided wooden bench—one that was supposed to have been repaired some time ago. Large, deep green bushes flanked both sides, sharp leaves poking at her shoulders. She folded her arms across her chest. "You said you would explain. Pray do so immediately."

Lady Russell—what else was she to call the creature?—harrumphed and gave her wings a little flap, pacing on tiptoes in front of the bench. "And I will. I am just trying to decide where to begin."

"Let us start with this. What are you?" Anne looked directly into Lady Russell's eyes.

Something about the expression was uncomfortably like her friend.

"I am a dragon. A species of cockatrix not native to England, to be precise."

"I read of those last night, but you look nothing like the pictures in the book." Was she really having this conversation?

"A rare species, as I said. Your mother and I used to laugh at the pictures in that book—assuming your father gave you the bestiary I am thinking of. While much of the information can be useful, the illustrator was dreadful. I suppose, though, he is not entirely to blame. There are actually quite a few species of cockatrice; we take a variety of shapes and sizes. So, there is no single image of my kind that would be correct. To complicate matters the male, cocks, and female, cockatrix, of our kind are of vastly different forms, so we are often mistaken for other creatures."

Anne pressed her temples. Too much information. "So, you are a cockatrix?"

"Yes. From Australia. I met my friend, Sir Henry, there, you see. We were so terribly close. He suggested I join him when he returned to England. Thus, I am here."

"But you have claimed to be Lady Russell, living as Sir Henry's wife. How is that to be? Dragon Friends, as I understand, persuade others to see them as animals of various sorts."

Lady Russell harrumphed and fluttered her wings across her back. "If you read your mother's book, you know—"

"I know dragons hide in plain sight, using their skills of persuasion to affect their disguise. But the text also says that those skills are limited to certain kinds of persuasions."

"Yes, yes, but my kind are particularly persuasive. We are said to be the most persuasive in dragonkind." She puffed out her blue not-quite feathered, not-quite-scaled chest.

"It seems you have been lying to me all my life."

"Not lying, dear girl. Those who do not hear dragons must be persuaded that they do not see them, either."

"This certainly seems an ill-advised sort of disguise." Nothing she had read addressed this sort of situation, but—

"Do not judge what you do not understand." Lady Russell stomped both feet and scratched at the floor. Her talons were particularly impressive. "It began as a bit of a lark, really, Sir Henry's idea for a spot of fun, to see how far I could take a persuasion. You see, I am able to persuade even the majority of dragon hearers—they do not seem to find it painful as you do. But it worked out so well that we could hardly stop once we had begun. If his wife suddenly disappeared—"

"But everyone on Kellynch has heard you speak whilst believing you to be a lady. I am quite certain few, if any, can hear dragons, yet you converse with everyone quite regularly. How is that possible?"

"Some cockatrix can affect a voice that even the dragon-deaf can hear. I have heard it described as similar to the way a parrot can talk. We are not dumb animals like birds, though, and are entirely aware of what we are saying, so it really is not the same sort of thing." She straightened her neck and pulled her wings back. "It is a trait that sets us apart from the rest of dragonkind entirely."

"I have just been presented to the Blue Order." Anne held up the signet, once her mother's, now engraved with a number that designated it as Anne's. "You know of them?"

"Sir Henry did but had little to do with them. They only complicate matters with their endless rules and articles and protocols. Besides, they are scarcely concerned with minor dragons like myself. Their primary concern is with the major dragons, the landed creatures who are apt to war among themselves and with men. That sort of thing causes far more harm than a relatively innocuous creature like myself." She pressed her wing to her chest.

"Even so, I am not sure it is a good idea."

Lady Russell shook her head, and the movement coursed like a waterfall down her long neck and back all the way to her tail feathers. "I do not recall asking your opinion. Clearly, you do not understand the nature of minor dragons." She clapped her beak and shook her head in broad swoops. "But who could hold you accountable for what you must not have yet been taught? Rest assured, I have duly presented myself to Kellynch and have submitted to his rule over this territory. That is really the important thing. In fact, he appointed me to act as his Watcher, what you would call a steward over his lands."

"Kellynch? You know him?" Anne gasped and gripped the bench with both hands. She might be the only living creature on the estate to have actually interacted with him.

"Of course! You have never been introduced? Well, no, of course not. Why would you be introduced when you did not hear dragons? Banish the thought."

"Kellynch? Introduced? You mean to say he is awake?"

"No, silly girl. I am sure you would have come into your hearing far sooner if he had been. His voice is so much more powerful than mine, you would have noticed him. He is still deep in hibernation." Lady Russell stretched her wings and pointed to the door. "Come, now that you hear dragons properly, it is time you should meet him. I am quite certain your father will never manage the task, so I will take you to see him and explain along the way."

Chapter 10

THE CREATURE—LADY RUSSELL as she would now have to accustom herself to calling it—no, not it, but her—gracious, this was all too much!—guided Anne out of the conservatory and onto a path that led into the deep woods where Anne rarely walked.

Large hardwood trees overhung the path, creating a dense, looming canopy overhead. Cool shadows enveloped everything, hushing the normal sounds of the woods. The place felt a bit dark and foreboding, not in the romantical sort of way one read about in novels. But in the sort of way that people of good sense kept away from—exactly why she generally avoided the place. The air, it carried a hint of the scent she had smelt in Bath—there was dragon in the air! Was it even safe to be following a dragon she barely knew into such a situation?

On the other hand, was it fair to say that she bare-ly knew Lady Russell? When was any of this going to begin making sense?

"Where to begin, where to begin," Lady Russell muttered, her wings ruffling in time with her musing.

"Does Father know you are ... what you are?" Anne wrung her hands as she hurried to keep up with Lady Russell's long strides. What unique footprints her talons left in the soft loam.

"I am quite certain that he does not. Though he hears dragons, he is not fond of them. He would much rather ignore us than acknowledge us. Since it is easier for him not to know my true nature, he is easily persuaded." Her head bobbed in time with her aggressive steps.

How well she understood Father. "And what of my sisters?"

"Elizabeth does not hear at all, which, if you ask my opinion, is a very good thing indeed. She has not room in her sphere for anyone more demanding than herself—which I will warn you, dragons are. Mary might; I think she will, eventually; but if she does, then she will be very much like your father. It would be no loss since she is as demanding as Elizabeth in her own way." Lady Russell was nothing if not an excellent judge of character.

Father could handle presenting Mary to the Order himself. "Dragons are demanding?"

"I am certainly not. But major dragons with land holdings can afford to be." Lady Russell glanced over her shoulder, eyes wide as though just a bit affronted.

"Are they dangerous, these major dragons?" These woods veritably dripped with the sensation that they were.

"Of course, they are! Why do you think there is a treaty to control their behavior? Left to their own devices, they will fight with each other over territory and with men over everything else, to take whatever is convenient." Why did the question seem to agitate her so?

"If they are so powerful, why would they adhere to something as ephemeral as a treaty?"

She stopped suddenly, but did not turn to face Anne. "Because they are not stupid. At least not most of them. They can see what is in their best interest and act upon that. Dragon wars are bloody, destructive things, and only the biggest, fiercest dragon wins. Everyone and everything else suffers—even the winning dragon after a time. And when dragons war with men," a shudder rippled down her back, her feathers making an odd rainfall sort of noise, "it is a truly awful thing."

"You have seen dragon war?" Anne shuddered. The description of the wars in the Blue Order books had given her vivid, gruesome nightmares.

"I hope never to again." Lady Russell snapped her beak and started off at a trot.

"Are there other major dragons near?" Why could she not recall what the Order's books had said about territory sizes?

"The next nearest dragon estate is Uppercross. But there are many scattered throughout England."

Wait, wait, what? Anne nearly tripped over a tree root. "Uppercross has a dragon?"

"The old wyvern is quite a character. I think you will like him very well, once you gain an introduction to him, that is."

"Does that mean …"

"Yes, yes, the Musgrove boy hears, but no, he does not know my true nature. Since your family believes me to be Lady Russell, it was not difficult to persuade him and his of the same. Uppercross agrees that it would not be a useful thing for him to know—far too easy for the wrong thing to be said in front of your father, complicating matters, and so the issue is settled."

"What about Wentworth?" Her heart raced harder against her tight chest. Did she even want to know?

"That is of little matter now."

"I do not agree. Tell me of him."

"Look, there. Can you see it?" Lady Russell pointed into the forest with her wing. "In the shadows of the undergrowth, that is the entrance to the lair."

Merciful heavens, dragons were stubborn! Anne squinted, breathing so hard that it was difficult to make out the shadowy tunnel in a hillside behind draping ivy.

"Kellynch has not been out in quite some time, which is why it is covered in vines. The entrance to the lair is usually kept more accessible."

"You have not answered my question."

"There are far more important matters right now." Lady Russell scratched the soft ground with her talons, kicking up dirt on Anne's skirt. "Have you been to a dragon's lair before?" She folded her wings across her back with much the same effect as a lady folding her arms over her chest. "There is an etiquette to these things that one cannot ignore."

"I thought he was sleeping."

"And the first rule of etiquette is not to wake a sleeping dragon."

"Then why are we here?" When would she start making sense?

Lady Russell hunched her shoulders and folded into her one-legged thinking posture. "Because he is accustomed to me coming and going and will not be disturbed by my presence."

"Why would you be coming here?" The leading edge of a headache teased at the back of Anne's neck. But not the same sort as before. Impatience fueled this one.

"I check on him periodically and attend to any need he might have, keep tail mites at bay and the like. As his Watcher—"

"What is a Watcher?"

"I monitor his territory and keep it running smoothly."

"The Order does not seem to agree." Anne squeezed her eyes shut.

"What would they know about Kellynch's affairs? Kellynch is satisfied, your father is satisfied, so why should they be bothered?"

All told, it sounded like exactly the sort of arrangement the Order would not be satisfied with. "Do you know why dragons hibernate?"

"Usually it is only when they are not happy—or very cold or facing some sort of danger that is better waited out than fought. Kellynch is the former kind."

At least that agreed with what the Blue Order had said.

"Kellynch thinks very little of Sir Walter, or of his father before him."

Perhaps that was why Father thought little of dragons. He did not like anyone who did not recognize his natural superiority. "So, the dragon is unhappy and sleeping now because of it, and one should not call upon a sleeping dragon." Anne clutched her temples and bowed her shoulders.

Breathe, she needed to breathe before the pressure in her chest burst forth in something truly untoward. "Pray then, tell me, why are we here doing just that? You must explain! How did you even become his Watcher when he has been sleeping?"

"I said one should not wake a sleeping dragon, not that one could not call upon one. There is a difference. I called upon him when I arrived. My scent roused him enough for us to make our agreement, and he went back to sleep, satisfied in all regards. And with respect to your other question, sleeping dragons will eventually awaken and when they do, they will need a Keeper to manage their needs."

"What of my father?"

"Officially, he is the Keeper, I am well aware. But there is little likelihood that he will be able to satisfy Kellynch's needs any better than his father before him. Where do you think he came by his attitudes?" Lady Russell made an odd sound deep in her long throat and chittered like an angry cat. "Unsatisfied dragons are grumpy, and grumpy dragons are not good for a territory. It is part of my duty to Kellynch to ensure there is a Keeper ready who will satisfy him. That was a condition of him accepting me as his Watcher, one he insisted upon most strongly. I did not know how it was to be accomplished—"

"Then why did you agree to it?"

"But now it is all very clear, and I could not be more pleased."

Anne pressed her eyes with thumb and forefinger. "The Blue Order Undersecretary said much the same. They want me to take the role of junior Keeper. But I have no idea how to do that. The books they gave me—"

"Are largely stuff and nonsense. I disagree with much of what they say and doubt most of the rest, and you should too. I will take you under my wing and make sure you are prepared to do what needs to be done. That is precisely why we are here now. I must begin your preparation immediately. It will take you some time to become adept in the skills of Dragon Keeping. You need to be ready when Kellynch awakes."

"I am not sure I want to do any of this." Anne whispered through her fingers, staring at the ominous lair.

Lady Russell stepped very close and looked into her eyes, nose to beak. "You must understand what is at stake. If your family does not fulfill its responsibilities to the dragon attached to the estate, Kellynch will complain to your precious Order who will remove your family from the estate and replace them with someone who will properly fulfill the duties."

"If you have known all this time, why did you not—"

"What could I do? Your father cannot be worked on."

"What if I cannot please this Kellynch dragon, and we are removed?"

"In all likelihood, the Order would ensure that society believed your father was selling the estate to pay off debt—"

"Debt? But there are no debt collectors at our door." Not that there was moderation and economy in the running of the house either, but ....

"I am relieved to hear that—it would be a serious issue if there were. But it matters little. The peers of the Order can easily make it believed that debt has caused your family's fall. Moreover, they will censure him within the Order and cut him in public, giving credence to the rumors. The Order prefers not to be forced in these matters, but they are very powerful. They will do what is necessary to maintain the peace for the good of all England. The fate of a single family pales by comparison."

Anne swallowed hard against the cotton wool gathering in her mouth. Did Father comprehend what he stood to lose? Probably not. It was not the sort of thing he generally attended to. When Father found something to be inconvenient, it simply ceased to exist. "Was Mama …"

"Kellynch was sleeping when she arrived, but she managed most of the other dragon estate affairs and did a sound job of it. And you are her daughter and heir to her legacy. I mean to make you a credit to her." Lady Russell made a funny little clucking sound in the back of her beak. "The first step is to allow you to experience for yourself the truth of the dragon in your midst and see Kellynch. And trust me, it will be far easier on you to do that whilst he sleeps."

Anne gulped.

"I will warn you, most of your kind find their first encounter with a major dragon rather overwhelming. Whatever you do, do not scream, do not cry out. It could be dangerous to startle Kellynch whilst he sleeps. Follow me." Lady Russell ducked her head and strode into the hillside opening with high, mincing steps.

Anne pressed her fist to her mouth, insides quivering like Father's favorite jelly, and pressed through the curtain of cold, prickly vines into the tunnel. The air was still and heavy, as though filled with cold fog. The darkness increased with each slow step. Her eyes slowly accustomed themselves to the dim light sneaking through cracks in the rock overhead.

What was the smell? Not quite what she had smelt in Bath, it was not precisely bad, but neither was it pleasant. Musky, with hints of manure and rotten offal. Overpowering, all encompassing, it filled the entire space with a presence all its own.

Somewhere in the distance, something wheezed—or was that snoring?—something quite large, indeed. How great a creature did it take to make a sound that echoed off the tunnel walls and reverberated in her bones?

"We are nearly there." Lady Russell whispered and reached her wing back to touch Anne's hand.

Several tiny fingers on the end of the wing clasped Anne's. She shuddered and pulled her hand away—it was too much right now to touch such an odd appendage—but followed close. Was it possible that the dim light was growing still dimmer? If this continued, she would not be able to go on.

Lady Russell turned and placed her beak very near Anne's ear. "There, if you look close, you can just make him out. He is curled up like a cat, his nose under his tail. There is a sliver of light on the highest point of his spinal ridge. If you follow that down, to the right you can just make out his head."

Anne bit her knuckle and squinted into the darkness. She found the splinter of light and followed it as Lady Russell directed, nearly gasping as an enormous somewhat leonine head came into focus.

The creature most resembled what the bestiary had called a wyrm—long and legless, like a snake with a squared-off head and a bony ridge along its back.

That was only a guess though, as the darkness obscured most details, not the least of which were his color and actual size.

Anne leaned against a rocky wall and slid to the floor, head in her hands. How could she have never known what lived in the hills behind her home? What would the residents of Kellynch do if they knew? No wonder the Blue Order demanded such secrecy.

After a few minutes, Lady Russell prodded her to her feet and led the way back out, saying very little until they reached open air, well away from the lair.

Anne stood in a brave sunbeam that had forced its way through the canopy. Leaning against a tree, she drank in gulps of fresh sweet air. Warm, yes, yes!— what was it about the lair that made her feel she might never be warm again?

"I have to say, I am impressed. Many faint dead away at their first encounter with a major dragon."

Anne covered her eyes with her hand. How quickly Lady Russell forgot Anne had fainted when she recognized Lady Russell's true form. "I may yet do just that."

"You have had quite enough for today. We should not tax you too much. Learning that your dear friend is in fact a dragon is quite a shock to one's system. Tomorrow, or perhaps the next day, we shall begin your instruction on being a Keeper. Right after you accept Charles Musgrove."

Anne's stomach flipped over in her chest. What a time to be reminded of the Blue Order's demands. "I cannot accept him."

"Of course, you can. You should, you must." Lady Russell stomped, her voice taking on that painful, raspy edge.

"Pray do not speak to me that way! It hurts!"

Lady Russell hopped back, eyes wide. "Yes, yes, I forgot, do go on."

"Accepting him is quite impossible. Do you not see?"

"See what? There is no impediment. If you marry him, you will—"

Anne pointed toward the hillside cavern. "You just introduced me to Kellynch—at least after a fashion you did. Charles is heir to his family estate and, I must assume, to the family dragon, Uppercross."

"He is not the family dragon. If anything, it is the other way around."

"Even so, Charles is committed to Keep that dragon—Uppercross. You have just told me that I am to be some sort of Keeper to Kellynch. If that is the case, how can I possibly marry a man committed to another dragon? The *Annals* I have been reading make it quite clear that major dragons do not share territories, which, I have to imagine, includes Keepers." While they did not explicitly say that, it certainly seemed the correct conclusion.

Lady Russell hunched onto one leg and turned her head nearly upside down. "I confess, I did not think of that."

"Am I wrong?

Lady Russell blinked several times. Her eyelashes were impossibly long over her dark, glittering eyes. "No, no, I do not suppose you are."

"Then say no more about my refusal of Charles Musgrove." Just like they did not talk about Fredrick Wentworth. What had been her role—

"I suppose this means that you must marry your father's heir ..."

Bless it all! The one thing she had hoped to keep from Lady Russell. "As you have said, I think there has been enough for today." Quite enough. Possibly too much.

Mr. Elliot would not arrive for at least a fortnight. Plenty of time to think things through before then.

Hopefully.

They headed back to the house, Lady Russell chittering under her breath her dissatisfaction at Anne's unwillingness to discuss Mr. Elliot. Maybe she would simply have to become accustomed to the sensation.

What sort of uncharitable thought was that?

One of the Order's monographs suggested associating with dragons changed one, but it did not detail in what ways. Could this sort of thing be what the author meant?

Was it a bad thing?

Perhaps it was too soon to tell.

11
Chapter

A WEEK LATER, Anne sat in Mama's room, curled in the striped, overstuffed chair, surrounded by the pink and yellow roses on the drapes and upholsteries. A sunbeam peeked over her shoulder, teasing and flirting with the words on the pages as light clouds danced across the sun. The breeze that propelled them wafted through the open window, carrying the perfume of late summer blossoms. The roses had long since faded, and though other blossoms succeeded them, nothing could replace their fragrance.

A modest writing desk, purloined from the guest wing, now replaced the small marquetry table that had once stood by mother's window. The books Mr. Wynn sent with her had overwhelmed the little table. Still, it stood just behind Anne's chair, receiving the overflow from the desk.

So many books! Not a few of them seemed arcane—who but a trained scribe could make sense of half of what was being said in odd riddles and verses? Between the faded, tiny print and the regular insertion of esoteric characters, they might as well have been written in a foreign language altogether. And of the ones that were legible, so many were either self-contradictory or in disagreement with other Blue Order publications. How was one to make any sense of them?

Mr. Wynn and Mrs. Smith had insisted that she write to them with any questions from her studies, but where to even begin such a correspondence without appearing lazy or stupid? She might not have the celebrated Elliot pride, but she was not without some level of self-respect.

Anne pushed *Greystoke's Bestiary Listing All Dragons Great and Small Common to the British Isles with Commentary upon the Habits and Habitats Thereof* to the side of the desk, careful not to knock off the three books piled precariously near the far corner. She flipped open her blue cloth-bound journal to the page where she had left her pencil. What was it she had been jotting there—oh yes, questions regarding wyrms. That was the sort of dragon Kellynch was supposed to be, or at least that was what Lady Russell had said. So much of what she said contradicted the books in new and different ways, distinct from the ways they contradicted each other, adding new layers of confusion to what she had been reading.

Anne's temples throbbed. What joy, her faithful companion headache had returned. What would be a morning study session without that?

"There you are! I have been searching the house for you!" The heavy paneled door flung open and banged against the deep rose-colored wall, leaving a dark mark where the doorknob struck the wall.

Anne jumped, her journal sliding to the floor. "Father! Pray forgive me, I had no notion you were looking for me."

"Studying again, Anne. Really?" He sauntered in, judgement following him like a shadow.

"I have so very much to learn, I can hardly—"

"Learn? It is unseemly for a woman to spend so much time studying. Look at you! It damages the posture, and I am sure it is not good for your eyes. You are squinting and will develop wrinkles far before your time. And the way you are clutching your temples every time I see you. That headache cannot be a good sign. I am certain all this bookishness will induce some sort of mania or brain fever if you continue as you are."

"I appreciate your concern, sir. But I am certain that I just need better light in which to read." And books that did not constantly disagree with one another.

"No, no, you must change your habits. I insist. You will stop this study altogether." He swooped to gather books from her desk.

Anne jumped up and blocked his way. "I cannot, Father. The Undersecretary explained it to you in Bath."

Father huffed and produced a wrinkled paper from the pocket of his coat, waving it as he stomped across the room. "Bath! Undersecretary of the Blue Order! I am so tired of this Order! I am quite ready to withdraw from it completely."

Deep breathing—that was what Mama always recommended for avoiding saying things one would regret. "I understand they are frustrating to you. But you know that is not a choice."

"How dare those people presume to tell me how to run my family!" He waved the offending paper.

"I have not the pleasure of understanding you. Pray tell me what is wrong."

"This!" He slapped the letter with the back of his left hand. "This is what is wrong. They have overstepped their boundaries—ridiculous muffin-faced, blubber-cheeked interfering, pompous—"

"What did they say?" If only she could snatch that paper from his hand and read it herself.

His face screwed up in a sneer that few but perhaps royalty could muster. "Regional Undersecretary Mr. Peter Wynn deigns to write to me to strongly suggest that the Blue Order would heartily approve of a marriage between my daughter and my heir presumptive—"

No! Anne winced.

"—my daughter Anne—" The way he said her name, he might as well have slapped her. "—and Mr. William Elliot. How have you contrived this honor?"

"I have done nothing! It is not a matter of honor, but a matter of Dragon Keeping. Elizabeth cannot; she is unable—"

"You have no business criticizing your sister. How dare you aspire to such a match! It is hers to claim, not yours."

"I do believe that Mr. Elliot does have something to say in the matter, does he not?" Where had that come from? Sarcasm probably was not a good idea.

Father glowered. "He will receive Kellynch someday. Why would he not want to see Elizabeth's dowry stay with the estate? It is a considerable sum. Any smart man would not wish to impoverish himself—"

"Elizabeth will be so flattered to hear you say that." How kind of him to offer the subtle reminder that Mama's legacy would not be equally distributed among her daughters. After all, it took far more to attract the attention of a titled man than just a mister.

He stomped toward her. "The honor of becoming a Lady—Lady Elliot—is due her as the eldest child of this estate! You are ruining her—"

"I have done nothing." Anne clutched the edge of the desk behind her. "This is not my choice, not my doing. None of this! The Order told me the same thing. It is my duty and would be advantageous to you."

"To me? Contravening my will is no favor to me."

"Your Dragon Keeping has not been—"

"I never asked for it. I have never wanted it. It is a burden I do not take gladly. It is the unfortunate baggage attached to our family, a curse, most unfortunate. Why am I to be criticized for a task I never asked for in the first place?"

"That changes nothing of the situation."

"I will not allow you to ruin all Elizabeth's hopes and aspirations. She should not have to leave her ancestral home. I will encourage nothing that will require that."

Anne took a deep breath and bit her upper lip, modulating her voice into something soft and nearly a whisper. "If I am mistress here, she would not—"

"There, you see, your ambitions are above your station. It is disgusting, and I will not have it."

"Yours are not the only orders I must consider."

He leaned very close to her face, so close she could feel his breath. "You would choose the Blue Order over your family, the very connections that should mean the most to you?"

"I choose the Blue Order in order to preserve my family. We are in a very precarious position, you must understand—"

"You would presume to tell me what I must understand? I should never have permitted you to assume the duties of a junior Keeper."

"You will recall what Mr. Wynn told you—"

"He said a great many things that I do not care to be bothered with, and I will not. Mr. Elliot will be arriving next week, and I expect you to behave appropriately. Elizabeth is a most appropriate wife for him, and you will do nothing to interfere with that. And should you choose to be willful and cross me, know that I will not give permission for you to marry him. What say you to that?"

"What can I say, sir?"

He snorted and stalked from the room.

She fell back into Mama's chair. Expecting that Father would suddenly embrace the Blue Order's requirements—no, that had never been a possibility. But grudging tolerance—she had hoped for that—but it had been a bit of a pipe dream.

Clearly, he expected her to do what she always did—accommodate his wishes, regardless of her own opinions. But how could she, when it meant the family could lose Kellynch entirely?

Saving the family meant she needed to marry and marry not just well, but to a very particular man. She wrapped her arms around her waist and leaned forward, her forehead on the desk.

Was Mr. Elliot even interested in marrying, much less as the Order might direct? How did one attract such interest? Merciful heavens! What did she know about attracting the attentions of a young man? Much less one with whom she was not even acquainted and was only interested in marrying to be of service to her family? And how could she hope to succeed against Elizabeth's charms and Father's favor?

September 1809

Over the next week, Elizabeth fluttered and fretted over Mr. Elliot's impending arrival. She took over many tasks, which usually fell to Anne, to ensure everything would be right for their guest. What matter that Anne knew much better how to manage the servants and their household tasks? Everything was certainly in better hands if Elizabeth managed it.

At least Anne had more time for her studies. Which she needed, considering how much time had already been taken up when Father forbade her from using Mama's room—did he believe that study could only be carried out in that room?

All the books sent by the Order had to be transferred to Anne's room. Naturally, the servants were all busy with Elizabeth's disorganized efforts, and Anne had to move them all herself, one by one, carefully avoiding Father or any who might report her activities to him, lest he try to wrest the books from her possession.

At least it gave her opportunities to study Mama's bookcases more thoroughly. Anne added a few of Mama's volumes—some which looked potentially very useful—to the formidable collection in her own chambers.

A bookcase would be required, but that would have to wait until after Mr. Elliot finished his visit and Anne could go back to managing the servants herself. In the meantime, most of the books could be kept in the trunk the Order had sent them in. Though it was tucked in near her chest of drawers, it extended into the room just enough that she kept knocking her shins on the trunk's sharp corner. Two gowns had torn as well—managing dragons—or at least preparing to—seemed hard on one's garments.

Anne laced her hands behind her neck and stretched, elbows brushing the sides of the over-stuffed chair. Would her neck and back ever be straight again? Father might have a point; so much study was hazardous to one's posture. She stood and rearranged the rose-vine curtains whose flowers matched the burgundy of her soft chair. The color was pleasing against the soft green of the walls. Cool and soothing in the midst of so much upheaval.

Half a dozen volumes vied for territory on the little round table by her window—some very slim monographs, others—rather substantial tomes—covered hatching, hibernations, genealogies, bestiaries, and histories. The dusty scent of old books overpowered the fragrance of summer flowers that used to fill her room. Her commonplace book lay open on top of an open journal, the two together taking up all the remaining space on the table. How soon could she have the writing desk from Mama's room moved into hers? Not soon enough.

Was there even a place for that and a bookcase in her bedchamber? Overwhelming, simply overwhelming. Was she ever going to learn how to accomplish all the duties that had been unceremoniously dropped at her feet? No, that thought was utterly ungracious and unkind—though it was utterly true.

She stared through her windows down to Mother's garden. Squinting, she could just make out the little divot in the beebalm plants where Beebalm made her home. They had been conversing quite regularly recently. The little dragon had become rather nervous about an unfamiliar cockatrice that had been raiding the dovecote and eaves. Apparently, pucks were prey to cockatrice. Anne shuddered. It was the way of things, according to the Order.

Beebalm's anxiety made her willing to talk to even a "very stupid girl" since she had taken up the role of junior Keeper and might have the wherewithal to help.

Minor dragons with Friends in the Order could be afforded the protections of the Pendragon Accords, but those that lived wild did so at their own risk. That risk could be mitigated by living under the auspices of a dragon estate, subject to the rule of a major dragon. Then, the smaller dragons would be protected as part of the dragon's Keep.

And therein lay the rub. The strange cockatrice had not obtained permission from the local major dragon. Now it was up to the Keeper to make it stop.

According to Beebalm, Father should be told and made to intervene. Anne guffawed—that was as unlikely to happen as him quitting Kellynch altogether and letting it to some untitled upstart. There had to be another way.

Perhaps she should request Lady Russell's assistance. Her role as Watcher to Kellynch's interests made her like a man's steward, able to act for him in legal matters, whilst the dragon slept. Or at least that is what *Dragon Hibernation: The Implications and Complications Thereof with a Look Toward Mitigating Damages and Avoiding the Necessity Altogether* stated.

But on the other hand, Lady Russell often disagreed with what that monograph said—so often that Anne stopped mentioning it altogether. She pressed her forehead against the cool glass. The volume was, after all, an old one, and probably as out of date as Lady Russell argued it was. Still though, it was what the Order had recommended she read, and it remained her best source of information.

Odd that Lady Russell seemed averse to the Order's information and more interested in actively avoiding their notice than following their regulations. Was it right to fully rely upon her? Who could tell, especially when what she said made sense, often more sense than the official works of the Order?

Still, it was difficult to trust her when she had never answered Anne's question about Wentworth.

Best not dwell upon that. Anne crossed her arms over her chest and rubbed her shoulders.

Perhaps if she made it appear that she was requesting Lady Russell's advice rather than implying that she needed to take action—that might work. She usually responded well to that, often taking on herself to do exactly what Anne hoped she would. Yes, that was definitely the way to manage Beebalm's concerns.

Right after she did her duty by her family and their house guest. She sighed, straightened the curtains and turned away from the window. Mr. William Elliot, heir presumptive to Kellynch, would be arriving shortly, if the note he sent was to be believed. Father and her sisters would be gathering in the drawing room soon, if they were not already there. Her pre nce would be expected. As would her capitulation to Father's orders.

Hopefully, she would have the strength to disappoint him.

With a brief glance at her dressing table mirror, she removed her fichu from her favorite pink muslin visiting dress and steeled herself for a trip to the drawing room. That felt more exposed than she would have liked, but the Order had made it clear, it was not simply about her preferences. Was this the right way to compete with Elizabeth? Who knew, but at least she could in good conscience say that she had tried everything she could think of, no matter the outcome.

Like Father's office, the drawing room was blue, and he disliked it. More than once, he talked of refitting both chambers, but with no proper mistress in the house to oversee the matter, it became a background complaint, muttered when there was no other source of dissatisfaction to trouble him.

The room was hardly the eyesore he proclaimed it to be. The robin's egg blue walls were fashionable and a fitting backdrop for portraits of cross Elliot ancestors that lined the two long walls in neat rows, looking down judgmentally upon all who entered their domain. Bright lilies filled bowls on the sideboard and tables, perfuming the air with their unique fragrance. The blue—something like the color of clouds before a storm—brocade furniture might not have been the newest style, but it filled the room with a certain formality that suited the Elliot pride. A harp nd pianoforte took up the far corner near the win-ws, with several small card tables and matching chairs in the opposite corner. Altogether it was a serviceable drawing room, enough to be recognized as the finest in the neighborhood—what more could Father ask for?

No, that was not a good question to ask. Newer, finer, grander—that was always what he wanted.

Elizabeth and Father, both on the verge of being overdressed for the occasion, sat on the long brocade couch near the windows, watching the drive for any sign of Mr. Elliot's arrival. Mary, somewhat less well-dressed, plinked out something on the pianoforte. Was she purposefully creating that awful noise so that she would not be asked to play for company and thus avoid missing out on any interesting conversation? It was the sort of thing Mary might do.

Heavens above! That was another cranky and ungracious thought. Somehow, she would conquer such things. Dragons would not change her. Absolutely not.

"There! Papa, look! It is a carriage. I am sure that it is he." Elizabeth stood and pointed out the window.

Mary left the pianoforte—sweet relief!—and minced toward the window, wrinkling her nose. How was it her rounded shoulders that left her looking absolutely dumpy escaped Father's criticism? "There is no crest on the carriage. How can you be sure whose it is?"

"It would be presumptuous of him to have a crest on his equipage. He is only the heir presumptive. Why would you expect such a thing?" Father did not rise, but sat up very straight, peering at the window.

"Who else are we expecting today? There is no one in the neighborhood who has a coach like that one. Therefore, it must be."

One, two, three …. There, like clockwork, Mary had to have her say and the bickering began. Lovely, just lovely.

Anne made her way to the pianoforte. Music, soft and soothing was in order. If it did not quell their argument, at least it would soothe her own nerves and while away the time until the occupant of the mysterious carriage arrived.

A quarter of an hour later, the butler announced, "Mr. William Elliot."

A young man stood in the doorway. He was a well-looking man who had enough of the Elliot countenance to be quite acceptable to Father and to Elizabeth. Medium height, medium build, his eyes a medium sort of brown just like his coat and trousers. Elegant in an ordinary sort of way that one would probably not remember well once he left the room.

"You have come at last." Father rose.

Mr. Elliot, high hat tucked under his arm, bowed deeply. "I am honored by your invitation, sir."

"May I introduce my daughters, the eldest, Miss Elliot." Father pointed to Elizabeth, wearing her new white-and-green-striped walking dress, and she curtsied.

"I am pleased to make your acquaintance, sir." Her voice was everything soft and refined.

"The pleasure is mine." He almost looked like he meant it.

"And her sisters, Miss Mary and Miss Anne." Father chin-pointed, and they curtsied.

Mary stood a little straighter. How subtle of him to introduce her younger sister ahead of her. It was not as though she needed an additional reminder of Father's opinions. He had been very clear, indeed.

"Ladies." Mr. Elliot bowed again, eyebrows slightly raised.

Interesting. Had he noted the slight, too?

"I shall call for refreshments, I am sure you are weary from your travels." Elizabeth glided toward Mr. Elliot. Her figure showed to best advantage whilst walking.

"You are too kind. Thank you." He strode past her toward the chair Father indicated with long confident strides, barely seeming to pay her notice.

Elizabeth's cheeks colored. Oh, she was not happy.

"Go on and play for us, Anne." Father waved her back toward her instrument.

So, he would keep her from the conversation. At least he was trying to be subtle about it, not sending her to supervise some task in another part of the house. That was something to appreciate.

She began to play, softly though. Did Father realize she could hear everything said in the room? Perhaps preternatural hearing had some advantages.

"Did you have your driver circle the property as I suggested?" She did not need to look to know Father's chest was puffed up and his chin held high, just waiting for compliments to be paid to Kellynch.

"I did. A very impressive view, just as you said." That could be genuine or patronizing—without a glimpse of Mr. Elliot's face, it was impossible to tell.

"One that could hardly be improved upon, I am certain." Was it possible to hear Father thumbing his lapels?

"I do not know that I share that sentiment. Everything could use some improvement."

"Indeed? How would you improve it?"

"That walnut grove, for example. Do you not think a Grecian temple would be more suitable?" Perhaps that was a smirk in his voice?

"Knock down the grove that has been part of Kellynch for generations to replace it with such a useless structure? Banish the thought."

"You did ask for my opinion."

Father snorted.

Anne screwed her eyes shut. That sound never boded well.

Elizabeth and several maids brought in trays of refreshments. Shuffling footsteps suggested both men went to attend Elizabeth. Thank heavens!

Anne finished playing. Dare she join the rest?

"I do not think your father liked my suggestions."

She jumped and turned.

Mr. Elliot stood behind her, plate in hand, taking a bite of a small sandwich. "Forgive me, did I startle you?"

That was hardly the material issue. "Do you often presume musicians are eavesdropping on your conversation?"

Had she really just said something so very bold? How was she to keep that daring in check now that it had been awakened?

He cocked his head just so and gave her such an odd look and smile. That ring on his little finger, it matched her signet! He wore it so openly, not like a shameful secret to be kept. Papa never wore his.

He glanced at her waist, her chatelaine. "There is no need for you to prevaricate with me, Miss Anne, even if your father refuses to acknowledge what he is. You and I are both big enough to own to it."

A response would be polite and appropriate, but

that would require words that she simply did not have.

"You have never met one of our kind in public, have you?"

Actually, she had, Mrs. Smith, but best not contradict him so soon in their acquaintance.

"That is rather quaint. I expect you are accustomed to pretending that you are as other girls, but you do not have to do so with me."

"I ... I do not know what to say."

"Then say nothing at all. It will be our secret. I see your sisters do not sport the same little bauble as you have. You are one of a kind then." Something about his tone, the tilt of his head; was he flirting with her?

Her cheeks flushed. Was she supposed to feel this way?

"Come, have something to eat. Join in the conversation. Perchance then something sensible might be said." He turned and beckoned her to follow.

Merciful heavens! Elizabeth was glowering from the other side of the room. Seething, really. Perhaps she should stay at the pianoforte.

But how would she accomplish what the Order demanded of her if she did that?

She rose and allowed Mr. Elliot to serve her a plate.

12
Chapter

MR. WILLIAM ELLIOT had been in residence four, or was it five days, now? On none of those did he please Father with his attitudes or his opinions. Nor did he please Elizabeth by delivering to her the attentions she thought were her due. In fact, he seemed to take some perverse pleasure in vexing her by including not just Anne, but Mary as well, in all conversations.

Mary enjoyed it, but Father did not approve. He called it an air of conceited independence, which was to say, he was not certain he could bend Mr. Elliot to his will. That left Father irritable and easily provoked, a game Mr. Elliot seemed far too fond of playing.

Is that why he continued to flirt with her every time Father or Elizabeth was about? Did she wish it was something more? Perhaps. Maybe. One should enjoy a bit of flirtation from the man she had to marry, no? Or was it better that it was all business?

That was a rather dismal thought, was it not? Just

the way to begin a day.

Anne sighed and paused at her dressing table. Best discard the fichu, again. Mr. Elliot seemed to respond well to that, even if it left her feeling a mite cold, and if it were possible, vulnerable. But she would do what she had to in order to save her family, even if they were totally unaware of her sacrifice.

Now she was adequately dressed—on to face the morning room.

Anne ventured downstairs. Instead of the sun's welcome, Elizabeth glowered from her seat near the door, a half-eaten plate in front of her. Two settings of used dishes flanked Elizabeth's sides. Most likely left by Father and Mr. Elliot. Elizabeth and Father had stopped keeping town hours since his arrival, that way they could join him for the earlier breakfasts he seemed to prefer.

The breeze through open windows wafted gentle floral perfume in to mix with the fragrance of the tea and coffee services set out on the sideboard. Despite the sunshine, dark clouds seemed to gather on the landscapes on the walls.

Why was Elizabeth so cross? Perhaps that her breakfast company had left her to her own devices?

While that behavior might be construed as rude, yes, gentlemen had business to discuss and sport to enjoy during the morning hours. It would have been unusual for them to keep company with the ladies so early in the day. Not that such a little thing as social convention would stay Elizabeth's—dare she think it?—overinflated expectations.

Anne slipped in and made her way along the round table, toward the chair nearest the windows and farthest from Elizabeth. Light clouds that hinted at a possible afternoon storm drifted past and changed the sky blue of the walls to something vaguely grey and disquieting, an effect somewhat offset by a platter of fragrant Bath buns just within reach on the marble-topped dark oak sideboard.

"You are quite the lay-a-bed this morning." Elizabeth's eyes narrowed over her teacup.

"This is quite my normal hour to come down-stairs."

"Mrs. Trent was looking for you."

"For me? Are you not handling—"

"It was not about the menus or entertaining our guest. There is a problem with a maid and a foot-man—" Elizabeth's eyebrows rose just so. "A disagreeable sort of affair. You are much more appropriate to manage that sort of thing. I believe that was her business with you."

Anne bit her tongue. Asking why she was the appropriate person to deal with distasteful things rather than the one who was acting as mistress of the house definitely would not improve the atmosphere in the room. She served herself a Bath bun and tea with extra sugar to sweeten her disposition.

"Speaking of things disagreeable…." Elizabeth donned the expression she used to send scullery maids scurrying.

Anne held her breath. One, two, three … she must contain her opinions. It was not as though she did not expect this conversation.

"You have developed a most objectionable and unseemly habit." Elizabeth drummed her fingers along the side of her teacup, the china tinking under her fingernails.

Probably more than one, considering that lying

was also an ugly habit. "I have no idea what you mean."

Elizabeth harrumphed. "Your behavior with Mr. Elliot. It is highly improper, and I would thank you to stop immediately."

Anne broke off a piece of her bun and placed it delicately in her mouth—an excellent way of keeping her remarks to herself. Just the right number of sultanas in the mix and a pleasing crunch of sugar on top.

"Have you nothing to say for yourself? Surely you realize how inappropriate you have been. Just look at you! You have not worn a proper fichu since he has been here. You have never done such a thing before. You are trying to distract him from paying attention to me."

Anne sipped her tea. It could stand to be a mite sweeter. And Elizabeth had not been wearing a fichu either...

"Do not ignore me!" Elizabeth slapped the table. "You know it is wrong for you to put yourself forward to Mr. Elliot. I am the elder sister. You have no right for anyone to look at you before I am suitably married. It was bad enough—"

"There is no need to mention—" That was low, very, very low. Anne pushed her bun aside, stomach churning.

If only she could tell Elizabeth—or anyone—how little she liked this charade of flirtation and how much she resented Mr. Elliot for forcing her to it. Why did he not merely get on with doing his duty by the Order? Why did he act as though he might make some other choice?

"—that sailor fellow made you an offer, knowing

full well that I was not married or even betrothed."

Of all people she did not want to think about now, Wentworth was at the top of the list. "You did not even like him. What should it matter to you?"

"The elder sister is married before the younger ones. That is how it is done in proper society."

"I do not see how it signifies—"

"That is the proper way that it is done, and it is the way it shall be done now."

"You do not understand—"

"Indeed, I do." Elizabeth planted her hands on the table and half-rose to lean toward Anne. "You have some perverse need to take precedence over me. I do not understand why you are unwilling to assume your proper role in this family—as my younger sister. I will not allow you to shame us so."

"Shame the family?" Anne tucked her hands under her thighs lest they curl into unladylike fists.

"You will stop putting yourself forward with Mr. Elliot. You have been utterly shocking, fawning over him, insisting he pay constant attention to you."

"To me? You and I have not been in the same drawing room, I think." Since when had exchanging pleasant conversation over a hand of cards become fawning? And the conversation had hardly even been that pleasant; a few amusing anecdotes about his trip to Derby on Mr. Elliot's part; a bit of tittering from Mary; and Father droning on about the lack of fashion to be found in that part of the kingdom.

Yes, he had been a bit flirtatious—not just toward her, but to Mary as well. Besides, responding to his questions was polite and appropriate behavior. And what had been required of her.

"I say, stop trying to defend yourself! You have

been utterly shameless. One might think you a lightskirt for all your coy looks and attention-getting devices. I insist you come to your senses, and put a stop to it."

"To what? What precisely am I doing wrong?" No doubt her sin was having attention paid to her whilst in the same room as Elizabeth.

"You leave me no choice but to speak to Father about it. I do not see why he has not already corrected you on the matter. I know he has watched and has been disturbed as I have. It must be his refined sensibilities that have kept him from rebuking you as he should."

Anne pulled pieces from her bun and arranged them along the edge of her plate. Three had no sultanas. That could not be good. "I shall quit the drawing room entirely then, and leave you to enjoy Mr. Elliot's company without me. Will that suffice?"

"Stop being petulant!" Elizabeth slapped the table with both hands. "Now, you have made me lose my temper. Why is it so difficult for you to see—"

"Pardon me, Miss," Mrs. Trent curtsied from the doorway. Probably trying to keep her escape route from Elizabeth's temper clear. "The master wishes to see Miss Anne in his bookroom right away."

Elizabeth rose and tossed her napkin on the table. "I am not finished with this discussion. We will continue once I have seen Father."

"Begging your pardon, but he wishes to see Miss Anne." Mrs. Trent backed away.

"Anne? Whatever for? Surely you are mistaken."

"No, Miss. I am entirely certain of it. He said Miss Anne."

"No, he did not!" Elizabeth stalked out, Mrs.

Trent barely dodging out of her way in time.

Anne rose and followed, slow steps dragging along the marble tiles in the long corridor lined with hall chairs placed for beauty, not usefulness. Elizabeth's strident voice echoed near Father's study. Anne stopped and closed her eyes, her hand resting on the back of Father's newest and favorite Trafalgar chair. No sense walking into that.

"You!"

Anne's eyes flew open.

Elizabeth backed her into the wall beside the chair, nearly knocking her into a large picture frame. "I do not know how you have contrived to make Father do this."

"Pray excuse me. Father requires my presence." Anne sidestepped, but Elizabeth blocked her way.

"I am not finished with you. He may not realize it, but I know how your artfulness goes beyond this house, too!"

"Enough! I will not hear—"

"You have somehow kept Lady Russell away, the one person who would unfailingly censure you! I am certain she would not approve of your behavior. When I tell her how far out of hand things have got, it will ruin your friendship with her. Then how shall you feel?"

Anne ducked around her and rushed to Father's study.

It would have been helpful to have Lady Russell here to persuade Elizabeth into a better humor. But her absence was utterly intentional, and necessary. The risks were too great. Who knew if she could persuade Mr. Elliot, or if he would keep her secret if he found out? That would have to be dealt with, but for now, just one dilemma at a time.

She slowed her steps to a semi-dignified walk. Had Father and Mr. Elliot been discussing the estate's dragon-based problems? How did Mr. Elliot feel, knowing he was heir to the land, but Anne, as the eldest dragon-hearing offspring, was heir to the Keepership? Or had he already come to grips with that and what it would take to satisfy the Order?

It was possible he would demand to be Keeper himself even though only Kellynch's assent, or a judicial action, could transfer the role to him. Might he and Father argue over that? It was possible, though not commonly done. According to Mr. Wynn, most Order members found the uncertainty and bother of dragon preferences and judicial actions strong enough reasons to contract a convenient marriage.

Had they already agreed to an offer of marriage? Her heart pinched against its racing. Marriage—it would be the right thing to do—even if Mr. Elliot was no Wentworth. She did not have to love him to marry him, though it would have been nice. This was for the good of her family, even if they did not understand. Anne knocked on the paneled study door, biting her lip.

"Come in, Anne." Father's tone—he was exasperated.

The door dragged over the thick blue, gold, and ivory striped carpet with a shush—was it trying to remind her to keep her opinions to herself? Quite possibly.

"Yes, yes, come in." Father beckoned impatiently.

The carpet, heavy matching drapes, and as much upholstered furniture as could reasonably fit in the room dampened the sound in the study. It made it better for contemplation, Father said. But contemplating what?

The books on the shelves that lined both ends of the room were a display of the Elliot wealth, not something that ever saw use. No, that was not entirely true. He did read the *Baronetage*. That volume was always open on the most prominent table near the fireplace.

"Good morning, Miss Anne." Mr. Elliot rose from his seat, a large gold brocade wingchair near Father's imposing oak desk, and bowed. His green coat, buff breeches, and boots suggested he intended to ride this morning, or at least occupy himself out of doors. He would probably be flattered to know he resembled a fashion plate she had recently seen in *A Lady's Magazine*.

Anne curtsied. "Good morning, sir."

"It is quite a pleasant morning, thank you." Why did Mr. Elliot appear so self-satisfied?

Father sat behind his desk while Mr. Elliot pulled a matching wingchair over for her. Anne sat and looked at Father.

He stared back, eyebrow raised. "Ah, yes." He pressed his palms on his completely bare, polished, and intricately-inlaid desk top. "You understand why I have asked you here?"

"No, sir, you have not yet explained."

"It is a disagreeable business, to be sure."

He intended to talk about dragons. She must not sigh.

"It is a difficult thing indeed, to be saddled with a great beast to take care of who adds nothing to the value of the estate."

She glanced at Mr. Elliot, but his expression remained rather neutral. "As I understood, the land belongs—"

"Stuff and nonsense, I say. Who can give precedence to a foul, cold-blooded creature that does nothing but sleep? I resent anyone, any organization, that would consider a beast of higher rank than a man." Father snorted and flicked his hand.

So that was why he despised all things related to the Order or dragons.

"I am ashamed that you will have to inherit such an estate, Mr. Elliot. My truest comfort is that these things are not discussed in polite society, and that no one of true worth need know."

Anne leaned forward just a bit. "But, do not most peers—"

"That is quite enough, Anne." He rapped his knuckles on the desk. "I do not wish to discuss it further. However, Mr. Elliot has expressed a wish to see more of that ... aspect ... of the estate. He should ... meet ..."

"Pray, would you take me to the dragon lair and introduce me?" Mr. Elliot blinked slowly as though it were the most natural thing in the world to be asking.

"Would it not be better for you to do so? You are the Keeper, after all." Anne tried to catch Father's gaze, but he refused, glowering.

"I have other matters to attend this morning. I trust you have nothing pressing? You may put off your morning calls to another day." He brushed imaginary dust from his pristine desktop.

Good of him to decide her priorities for her. She tipped her head, teeth clenched. "I will do what I can, sir." Now was not the time to explain that one did not wake a sleeping dragon. "Pray allow me to fetch my bonnet, and I will take you there." And devise a way to explain to Mr. Elliot he was not to disturb Kellynch in the process.

A few minutes later, they stood enjoying the mid-morning warmth near the multicolored snapdragon border of Mother's garden, surveying the estate. In the distance, Shelby chased a few errant sheep back into their field. Overhead, the local harem of fairy-dragons twittered against the pale grey clouds shadowing the sun. She still did not know their names, but their colorful flights were very familiar. How peaceful and normal it all had seemed before she became aware of the true nature of the place. Now it was mostly peaceful, but hardly normal.

"So, what do you know of dragons, sir?" She did not look at his face.

"Enough to have this." He pointed to his signet ring. "I became a member in my youth, before I attended university."

She pressed a hand to her burning cheek. No doubt he knew far more than she.

"I am far more familiar with the smaller varieties than I am with the large ones, though. I have never actually met a major dragon in its own lair before. I think the prospect is rather exciting." He rubbed his gloved hands together.

"But you have encountered a major dragon before?"

"I have seen them at the Blue Order. When I was inducted into the group, in London, the Minister of Keeps, Sir Carew Arnold and his wyvern dragon Langham attended. Uppity, smelly old beast. I do not spend much time there, nor do I care to, if I were to be entirely honest." He snorted under his breath.

"You do not care for dragons?"

"I can see the value in the lesser creatures. They can be rather useful, to be sure. But the large ones? I share your father's sentiment. They are parasites on the land."

Lovely, just lovely.

A short distance away, a creature screamed.

That was Beebalm! Anne dashed toward the voice. Mr. Elliot pelted along the sandy garden path behind her.

Beebalm shrieked again—a sound more of terror than of pain. A dark hulking shape, rather like Wincombe, thrashed through the stalks of bee balm, showering pink and purple petals onto a huddling green-brown mass with frill extended.

"Stop! No more of that!" Anne stopped a wingspan away, her heart thundering loud enough to drown out her own voice.

The dark shape looked over its shoulder. Sunlight glinted off a sharp black beak and glittering jet eyes. Shiny ebony feathers covered its broad wings and trailed down its back into a glistening black serpentine tail. It hissed, first toward Beebalm, then at her.

"Leave her alone!" Anne stomped a little closer, crushing a stalk of violet beebalm.

"Who are you to command me?" The voice was thin, and sharp, and ruthless.

"Who are you who trespasses here?"

The creature—a cockatrice was it?—flipped its long wings to its back. "I do not owe you my name, but I am Jet, and there is no trespass."

"You have Kellynch's permission to be here?"

"Kellynch is of no authority whilst he sleeps." Jet

cawed and flapped—was it to give the impression of being larger than he was? One of the books said something—

"This territory is his, awake or asleep. You are trespassing."

The creature took three menacing hop-steps toward her and extended its neck. Beebalm squawked and dove for her hole.

"I do not recognize your authority." A musky, feathery dragon scent wafted toward her.

"I am junior Keeper here, daughter to Kellynch's Keeper."

Jet hopped two steps back and puffed out his chest. Maybe now he recognized authority?

"I suspect you have been hunting our doves and chickens. Without permission."

Jet snarled. "I must eat."

"That is trespassing as well." Anne folded her arms across her chest lest Jet, or Mr. Elliot—why was he not helping her?—could see her hands trembling.

"What are you going to do about it?" Did Jet just spit at them?

"Give you an opportunity to stop trespassing and escape unscathed." Pray he did not call her bluff.

"And if I choose not?"

"I will employ the assistance of a bigger dragon than you—several of them perhaps—to put an end to your violation of Kellynch's territory." Heavens above! Hopefully that was a correct answer.

"And who do you think will stand up to me? That stupid drake Shelby?"

"I have a certain cockatrix in mind who would not take kindly to poaching …."

Jet hopped back, his head bobbing toward the

ground. "There is no need."

Mr. Elliot stepped forward. "Absolutely! There is no need to further trouble this family or this estate. Listen to the good lady and remember your place."

Why had he waited so long to intervene?

Jet flapped at Mr. Elliot and snapped, "What rank have you here?"

"I will be master of this estate one day, and I have no need for creatures of your ilk."

Interesting, he said master, not Keeper.

"You are nothing to me." Jet's head swung back and forth as he approached Mr. Elliot.

"But you should not ignore me." Anne tried to glower, but as unfamiliar an expression as it was, it was probably unimpressive.

Jet cocked his head and pulled his neck back in something very much like a sneer. "What then can I eat?"

"What is wild in the woods and not dragonkind. I know you are apt to prey upon other dragons, but you may not do so here." That was the typical stipulation to minor dragons on an estate, at least according to Lady Russell. Pray she was right.

"No fairy-dragons? They will overrun the place."

"They have enough predators in the hawks and stoats and foxes here. You will not eat anything— anyone—that can speak back to you."

Jet's eyes narrowed. Hateful creature.

Bold, she was supposed to be bold. How was that to be done? "No. I know that look, and no. Do not attempt to find any loophole, make any wordplay with what I have said. My meaning has been made clear to you. I will not have you playing games with me."

Jet growled under his breath. "I do not appreciate—"

"Trespassers and poachers are not asked for their preferences; they are usually hung—or eaten. Be off with you now, and let the next time I see you be under better circumstances. Go!" She waved him away, arms wide.

Jet growled, stomped, flapped, and flew away. Perhaps she should have turned him off the estate altogether. But without the aid of Lady Russell and Shelby, she could not ensure he did not trespass.

Mr. Elliot stepped near her shoulder as they watched him fly off. Her head spun, knees growing more unsteady by the moment. Had she really just faced down a dragon—a minor one, but a dragon nonetheless? She staggered to the nearest tree and clung to it for strength. Hopefully that was a normal reaction for one's first hostile dragon encounter.

Mr. Elliot followed her. "Is that sort of confrontation commonplace?"

"No, it has never happened to me before." She panted heavily. "And I would be quite happy if it never happened again." Sweat trickled down the back of her neck, and she shivered.

"It seems you handled it quite masterfully." He stroked his knuckles along his jaw, shadows from the windblown clouds playing across his face.

"Then it is by luck alone that I happened into the right thing."

"You said something about a cockatrix. Might you introduce me to her?" There was something disconcerting in his eyes.

"She ... she is accepted by Kellynch but does not wish to be widely known. Perhaps at another time, I might ask her permission to make an introduction, but I do not think she would be amenable now."

"And that matters?"

"Do you wish to have acquaintances force upon you?"

"I had no idea such things mattered to the creatures." His lips wrinkled into a faint sneer.

"Courtesy is appropriate toward everyone in society." How could he not understand such a basic notion?

"Then I will contain my disappointment. You were quite impressive just now. Tell me, do you show the same mastery of the estate dragon as you did that one?"

"Hardly, I have not even met him. One does not wake a sleeping dragon, you see." She met his steady gaze.

"I did not. That is useful to know. It seems there will be no introductions today. Will you at least show me the lair?"

"I will, but pray do not ask me to take you inside. I think I have had enough of dealing with dragons today." Enough for an entire month at least.

"Very well." He offered his arm, and she took it.

13
Chapter

It was not like walking on Wentworth's arm—his was strong and warm and steady. Secure and trustworthy. Mr. Elliot was stiff and well—very proper and cool. But she needed the support and could hardly complain about what was offered, meager and unsatisfying as it might be. Would marriage to him be like this?

The path to the lair loomed a bit darker and more foreboding than it was the last time when she and Lady Russell had come. The canopy of hardwood limbs—surely, they leaned closer and heavier than before. Above them, dark clouds gathered, not quite ready to rain, yet. But soon. No birds sang in the trees, and nothing small and furry and warm-blooded scurried about, almost as though they knew a hungry, black predator was loose in the woods.

A shiver snaked down the back of her neck. Hopefully Lady Russell would agree she had handled the matter correctly or at the very least reassure her she had not made a total cake of things.

The trees parted to reveal the vine draped hillside. "There." She pointed. "The opening is behind the vines. There is a long tunnel to his den."

Mr. Elliot stared, shaded his eyes and squinted into the viney curtain. "Very interesting. Do you know if it is a single chamber, or many in that cavern?"

"I am not sure, but it is possible there are many. Why do you ask?"

"Just curiosity. There is little written, at least that I have found, on dragon lairs. Knowing what is part of the estate seems appropriate. In that vein, have you ever seen the Blue Order charter that assigns your family's lands to that dragon? I would like to know the legal obligations the estate has to the beast we are burdened to support."

"As I understand, our family was assigned to the dragon's lands." She tried to sound tentative and meek, but there was nothing tentative about it—the Pendragon Treaty and Accords stated it very clearly.

"Pish posh, scaly old lizards do not have precedence. They owe it to us for allowing them to live. If you ask me, they should be asked to pay for the privilege."

Best ignore the latter remark altogether. "I do not know that there is a copy on the estate. Would not the Blue Order keep such a thing?"

"I expect you are correct, but I would rather not trouble their record keeper if it is something that I can lay my hands on here." He glanced over his shoulder toward the manor.

"You might ask Father. He usually keeps important papers in a locking box somewhere in the house. What do you—"

"I hate to trouble him since he is so averse to all matters related to the Order. Perhaps you ...."

"I told you, I do not know where it is kept. You heard that he has no wish to discuss such things with me. If you want to know more, you must ask him yourself. What do you wish to learn?"

"Of course, forgive me. Shall we return to the house?" He offered his arm again. "How do you feel about dragons, Miss Anne?"

She shook her head and began walking toward the house, arms around her waist, stomach churning. "They seem decent enough creatures all in all, though I am barely acquainted with the Blue Order world. Forgive me if I observe that you do not seem well-disposed to them."

"When you get to know the Order, you will find there are more who believe as your father and I do than you would imagine." Could he be right? Had Lady Russell any idea of his opinions?

"I am surprised. I would have thought that members of the Blue Order would be amenable to dragons on the whole." The Smiths certainly had been, even without a companion dragon.

"It only shows your delicate, feminine nature that you would believe that. A rather pleasing trait, I think."

Such generous condescension. Her insides pinched and bitterness rose in the back of her mouth.

His steps fell a little more heavily. "All things considered, you do seem rather well versed in the management of the creatures."

Anne cringed. That tone of voice only meant one thing ....

"I know it is quite forward of me, our acquaintance so brief, but pray, might I ask a favor of you?"

"What do you require?" Good that he did not know her well enough to suspect the meaning of her tone.

"Oh, I do fear this is going to make me sound like quite the cad. I will have to trust in your good nature to hear me out and not to take unnecessary offense."

Cold prickles raced along Anne's cheeks. She would restrain her offense to the necessary variety only.

"I am sure you are all that is amiable and kind—it would be preferable to attach myself to a daughter of the estate who is to be Keeper, to be sure. In fact, the Blue Order has been so kind as to inform me of this in several missives of increasing severity. Perhaps you have received them too?"

"No, I have not, though one of the Order officers did mention something of the like in conversation with me. I believe my Father has received such a letter, though." How mortifying! Even Charles' plain and practical proposal was better than this.

"And what is your opinion of their demands?"

"I do not really know what to think. Our acquaintance has only been a week in duration, less than that really. That does make it all difficult. But I am told that marriages have been arranged for far lesser reasons." She shrugged and lifted open hands. Gracious, what a habit lying had become. That had to change immediately.

"I do know what I think. Pray permit me to tell you."

Something in his tone of voice ... she was not going to like his opinions.

"I know it sounds quite terrible to say this, but I have been told I have a decidedly independent streak. I have never liked to be told what to do in any facet of my life. I have always insisted on having the freedom of my own choice, and I will not do differently here for all that your father believes he is the master of all he surveys, or that the Blue Order believes they can dictate my life."

"My father?"

"He has been rather unsubtle in his intimations that I should marry your elder sister. If I understood his implications correctly, he even suggested that he might increase her dowry rather substantially in order to keep the money with the estate."

"I had no idea he would resort to such measures."

Mr. Elliot chuckled, but it was a disapproving sort of sound. "It was rather an interesting tactic; however, even that substantial a bribe is not enough to turn me from my course of self-determination."

"I hope you do not want me to broach the topic with him. That would be utterly unthinkable."

"No, certainly not! What must you think of me? I suppose I should come out with it quite directly. You see, I am already set upon a matrimonial course."

"You are betrothed?" Had the Order been aware when they made their demands?

"The announcements have not been made but will be soon. I needed to secure her father's approval—he is very interested in seeing me inherit Kellynch."

"You came to confirm that my father is not contemplating marriage."

"You must think me quite a brute. But, yes, her father insisted upon my confirmation of that fact." Mercenary.

"Does my father know you are for all intents and purposes, betrothed?"

"I will tell him before I leave."

"I imagine she is an heiress of some sort." Otherwise why would he ignore Elizabeth's doubly handsome dowry?

"You make it all sound so cold. We are really quite fond of one another." He winked.

"I am glad for you. Both of you."

"I hoped you would say that." He rubbed his hands together briskly. "You see, there is the small matter of the dragon. She does not hear them."

"All fondness aside, do you think it prudent to marry a woman who does not hear dragons when you will be the master of a dragon estate?"

"I will not be the first or last man to have done so. It can be managed. I know the Order does not prefer the arrangement, but you know I am not impressed with them. Besides, I fully expect that the dragon will continue to sleep under my tenure as it has for your father and his father." That was to say he fully intended to maintain the family tradition of terrible Dragon Keeping.

"Are you aware that a hibernating dragon is a troubled one? The Order is already concerned over what may happen when he awakens and finds that the situation has not improved. Planning to continue as things have been may be a very unwise strategy, indeed. In fact, if the dragon awakens—"

"Exactly, Miss Anne, that is precisely what I wanted to speak with you about. You have such an understanding of these things. I need your help. I understand all major dragons require Keepers. You are currently an apprentice, or is it junior Keeper for

Kellynch."

"Junior Keeper."

"The letters I received from the Order suggested that you will be integral to keeping the dragon in good order when it awakens and into the future as you are heir to the Keepership."

"I have been given the same understanding. The Keepership passes to the eldest hearing child, regardless of who inherits the estate. That role can be reassigned to another, possibly to the heir of the estate, if the dragon finds it acceptable. Forgive my candor, but I do not see—"

"Oh, no I do not want that role myself. I am quite content that you have it."

She clenched her teeth, neck and face growing hot. "But you have already said you have plans to marry another."

"Who says that I have to marry you for you to be Keeper of the dragon?"

"Excuse me? I have never read of such a thing."

"We are in modern times, Miss Anne, and the Order must keep up. Not all of us burdened with hearing the cold-bloods desire or even need be bothered with them. This is my plan: I will marry my betrothed, and we will live in the manor when I inherit Kellynch and you inherit the Keepership. I will see you have a cottage here and remain under my protection—"

"Wait, stop. Remain under your protection, like a mistress?"

"I will see you are cared for and in return you can Keep the dragon."

She stopped and turned to face him. "You propose to set me up as some sort of mistress to manage the dragon?"

"Exactly, brilliant is it not? Your future will be completely settled and the lizard's requirements will be met. How could the Order object?"

In so very many ways! Separating the Keepership from ownership of the estate? What would that do to the lines of inheritance alone? "And just how long will it be before you begin to make other demands upon me to earn my keep, as it were?"

His jaw dropped, and he edged away from her, but he was trying far too hard to look innocent.

"What if I should decide I wish to marry myself. You do not think my husband would be—"

He laughed, bitter and cruel. "Marry, you? I know you have already turned down two men. Do you really think anyone else will offer for you, especially when your father is so willing to impoverish your dowry for your sister's sake?"

"How would you know such a thing?"

"Fairy dragons hear everything and tell it all over and over again. Horrible gossips. Perhaps you should not have been so quick to protect them from that cockatrice. I would not mind seeing them banished from the estate altogether."

"That is not your decision to make. It is the estate dragon's."

"How would I know such a thing? That is why I need you to Keep the dragon."

"As a kept woman."

"It sounds so vulgar when you put it that way." He rolled his eyes.

She pulled her shoulders back very straight. "I am a lady, Mr. Elliot, not a ladybird. You will treat me as one."

"You are a lady with a very uncertain future. I am offering you one of comfort and stability. One that will allow you to do your duty to your family and to satisfy the Blue Order."

"No. You offer me only insults and speculations. I was barely willing to consider becoming your wife, sir. I will not be your mistress, no matter what the terms. That is a disgrace to me, to my father, to the legacy of Kellynch Hall. I will not have it."

"Really?" He tsked under his breath. "I had no idea you would be so determined. I had heard otherwise about you."

"I do not wish to know what you heard."

He lifted his chin and intoned in a falsetto, "That you were a sweet, obedient woman who would do whatever was required of her for the sake of duty and family."

"I will not be moved, sir. Pray leave me." She gathered her skirts and took off at just less than a run toward Kellynch Cottage.

He did not follow.

Had he truly just made her that disgusting offer? What would the Blue Order think of such a thing?

Did it really matter how the Order would consider it? Was it possible they could require that of her? She shuddered.

No! Absolutely not! Mr. Wynn said the Order would not force a marriage, so surely, they would not require something so far beneath her. Even if they did, she would refuse. She had rejected a respectable offer from dull, stable, respectable Charles Musgrove. She was not going to turn around now and accept such an … an affront from Mr. Elliot, no matter what his relation to the estate, the Blue Order, or anyone else.

She stopped near a fence stile and braced herself against it, gulping air like a drowning man. Something warm and malleable drained away from her chest. She pulled her shoulders back and spine tall; something firm and steady held her up—was that resolve? Yes, it was resolve. She could be, she would be, resolved.

Resolved to make the best of things. Resolved to manage the dragons of the estate as best she could. Resolved to become an active part of the Blue Order, an organization that was willing to see women as rational creatures, valuable in their own right. Resolved to never consider men or marriage ever again.

She did not need marriage to secure her future—she had the hope of dragons.

14
Chapter

Off the south coast off England, Late September 1809

CHOPPY WAVES SLAPPED at the hull, dancing in the light of the full moon. Beneath his feet the *Laconia* bobbed and swayed as it always did, steady and reliable. Streaky grey clouds drifted past the stars, never obscuring, just dancing flirtatiously among them. Chill and briny, a light breeze nipped his ears and nose. Winter would be along soon, with its cold and storms. Definitely not his favorite season, and it probably would not be Laconia's either. Being cold blooded had its limitations.

He might need a nest near the galley where he could keep warm. Cook would not mind. Not only did he like cats, as it were, but he was convinced that Laconia was the best mouser he had ever seen, and lucky to boot. Chances were good he would see hosting Laconia as a privilege, and if he did not, Laconia would persuade him he did.

Wentworth ran his tongue along the roof of his mouth. He still tasted Mrs. Harville's perfume, even though hours had passed since he had last seen her. Did she really have to use so much of it? Gah! Flowers, which a man should definitely not be eating, and other things he could not name. Perhaps he should speak to her about it, but no, one probably did not have that sort of conversation with a woman to whom he was not related.

She, her sister, and her cousin had been so excited to board this morning, so ready for their journey to Plymouth to join Harville there. Unfortunately, it was utterly impossible to make shipboard conditions suitable to a party of ladies. Still, the Harville ladies put forth a great effort to disguise their disappointment upon discovering how few comforts would be available whilst they traveled. That certainly won them favor among the crew.

Mercifully, their discomfort would be of short duration.

The efforts were worth it, though. He would assist any brother officer that he could with whatever he could. Moreover, he would bring anything of Harville's from the world's end, if asked. But that did not mean he did not feel it an evil.

At least there were several sea dragon pods in these waters and tantalizing hints of other, larger dragons they had not yet met. That should not thrill him as much as it did.

"Mrrooow." Laconia jumped up on the railing and approached, moonlight glinting off his shiny black fur and scales. How did one describe a gait that involved two nimble feet mincing across a rail and one muscular tail wrapped around it? Odd. That was the only word that came to mind. No, not just odd, but effective.

"You have left the ladies' company?" Wentworth reached out to offer a scratch.

"They have retired for the night."

"You do not sound as though you enjoy their doting and attention."

"Pffft." Laconia snorted and sneezed as he moved into Wentworth's reach.

"You do not like their perfume, either?" He did smell rather like Mrs. Harville now.

Laconia tightened his tail on the rail and shook, starting at his nose and rippling down all the way down his furred front half. "I dread what it will take to rid myself of the stench. I can hardly smell anything else."

Wentworth chuckled and scratched behind Laconia's ears as the little tatzelwurm leaned into his chest. How easy Laconia made it to forget he had ever been lonely. Even so, it was difficult not to wonder—

"You are thinking again. It is never a good thing when you begin thinking." Laconia pulled back a little and looked him in the eyes.

Wentworth dodged his gaze. "It is nothing worth bothering about. There are far more interesting things to discuss. Tell me of your conversation with that pod of little serpent-whales we saw this morning."

Laconia looked over his shoulder out over the choppy seas and sniffed. "Most of them had all the sense of that fluffy yellow fairy dragon you allowed aboard with those smelly females." He cleaned behind his ears with his thumbed paws—both at once. "but their lead female had some sagacity. She warned of a storm front coming in this direction and mentioned that there are other pods not far from here. I am hopeful they might have something a little more useful to say."

"Can we avoid it—the storm I mean?" If the tatzelwurm had weathered a few more serious storms he would value the serpent-whales' storm warnings far more.

"Already talked to the Ship Master about it."

"Quite the resourceful sailor, are you not?" Was it odd that his ship's cat was the most efficient officer onboard? "Does the Ship Master know from where your information comes?"

"Do I look stupid to you? It is already asking a great deal of him to trust one of my kind—I am quite tired of the bias against us, by the way. Spring-hopping does not addle our brains. The Ship Master would never put stock in intelligence from dragons he does not know."

"I suppose it is a lot to ask of even a dragon hearing man."

Laconia slapped the tip of his muscular tail against the smooth railing. "I am glad you got rid of that deaf one. Persuading him to change course was tiresome."

"You do not have much patience for the dragon-deaf, do you?" He scratched under Laconia's chin.

"Nor for dumb dragons who seem to think they are fine ladies and the weather is the only fitting topic of conversation."

Wentworth snickered. "You do realize that even if the only information we can get from the sea dragons is weather reports, it is worth our efforts. How much the navy would save not being blown about by storms."

"Your standards for satisfaction are very low, I think. I know there are more intelligent dragons out there." He pointed into the distance with this thumbed paw. "Ones who know more and understand the value of their information. And when we find them and bring them into union with us, the return will be great for both sides."

"You have such big dreams my little Friend."

"Do you not believe in them?"

"When I hear you talk about them, I do."

Laconia wrapped his tail around Wentworth's waist. Comfortable silence fell between them, broken only by the lapping waves and Laconia's purr.

"You are thinking again."

"It is nothing, let it be."

"You have been thinking a great deal." Laconia sniffed Wentworth's wrist. "You have not been the same since Easterly mentioned Kellynch."

Wentworth's stomach clenched. "Easterly mentioned a great number of things during that conversation."

"Yes, but you did not smell different until he mentioned Kellynch."

Smell different? Preposterous. "I do not want to talk about it."

Laconia rose up on his tail and ran the top of his head under Wentworth's chin, purring a little louder. "Those females you have brought on board. You have fretted ever since they arrived."

"I just want to see them properly cared for, just as I do with you." Laconia's fur tickled his nose.

"Do you like them?"

"They are Harville's family. For that they are important to me."

"But do you like them?" Laconia pressed his nose to Wentworth's. So persistent!

"Why do you ask?"

"The stinking one, she is your friend's mate? You will need to take a mate, too, I expect."

When had Laconia begun worrying about such things? He was still full young for it. "I suppose, it is possible, but it is not something that is on my mind right now. What are you worried about?"

"The other two females in the party, they do not hear. The little fairy dragon told me they are very stupid and rather useless. Why would a man who hears have deaf ones in his household?" So, his dislike of the dragon deaf ran deeper than it first appeared.

"Well, while one can choose his mate, the family that comes with that mate one cannot choose, rather like his own family."

"Have you other family? Can they hear?" Laconia swished his tail. Would that he kept it wrapped around something stable!

"Never you fear, my sister Sophy and her husband both hear. You know that. As to my brother, the curate, whom we have not spoken of, his Friend is a small puck whom many perceive as a pug with a peculiar attitude."

Laconia's tail wrapped around the railing again, and he seemed to sigh. "So, yours is a proper family, then."

"I am not sure anyone has ever called us that, but if you see us that way, I shall be grateful for the compliment. I look forward to your making their acquaintance."

Silence once again as the *Laconia* dipped and rocked soothingly beneath their feet.

Laconia bumped the top of his head against Wentworth's chest. "Would you take a mate that could not hear dragons?"

"I have no plans to take a mate any time soon."

"But when the time comes, would you?" Laconia did not meet his gaze.

"You do realize that there are precious few who can hear dragons? I have selected as many as I can for my crew here, but in the wild, as it were, I think it is less than one in a hundred who enjoys the privilege of hearing dragons."

"Even so, why would one with a Friend choose a mate who cannot share in that Friendship?"

"As I understand it is a commonly done thing, especially when there is no major dragon's keep involved."

"Well I do not approve." Laconia ducked under Wentworth's arm and slithered along the railing—his version of pacing. He grumbled under his breath and crept back to his original place. "I do not want to live with a dragon-dumb—"

"You mean deaf."

"The dragon-deaf are usually dragon-dumb as well. I do not like stupid, as you well know."

That was an understatement to say the least. Wentworth swallowed back a belly laugh.

"This is not a matter of humor. I am very serious. I do not want to live with anyone stupid. Your mate will have to hear dragons," Laconia looked him in the eyes, voice low, almost a growl, "or I will not stay."

Laconia would leave him?

Wentworth blinked several times, ice coursing through his veins, and swallowed back bile building at the back of his tongue. "I cannot have that happen."

Laconia exhaled and leaned heavily into Wentworth's shoulder, purring a low deep rumble that always meant relief.

"When that time comes, you may rest assured that I will seek your approval before I make any woman an offer of marriage." He wrapped his arm across Laconia and laid his hand on his head.

Prickly toes kneaded Wentworth's shoulder. "That is your promise?"

"Yes, you have my word."

Laconia stood on tip toes and he licked Wentworth's cheek with his raspy forked tongue, his entire body rumbling with the force of his purr. "Good."

Wentworth scratched Laconia until he pressed tight to his chest. Few would believe a mere tatzelwurm capable of feelings so deep.

What woman could ever give him this kind of unquestioning loyalty? How many women were there in the world who would meet Laconia's approval?

Anne Elliot.

No, he did not want to think of her again.

And yet, she was such a woman, even if her character was—or at least had been—so easily persuaded.

He had changed so much since those days. For worse in some ways, true enough. But definitely for better since befriending Laconia.

Was she altered, too?

What was she like now? Had she become less spineless, more steady? The makings of it were there, it just needed to be nurtured. She might be a very fine woman now, if there were someone to encourage her in it.

But Easterly had said Kellynch was troubled, the dragon sleeping. If Anne were aware of any of those troubles, she would be managing the matters and things would be handled properly. There was none so capable as Anne. Steady, sensible, sensitive Anne.

The woman who had broken his heart … no he would not go there.

Since Kellynch was in a muddle, there was no doubt: she was not involved in the dragon keeping. And that could only mean one thing.

Probably just as well. What point was there in digging up the tenderness of the past? Even if he could set aside his resentment, just or unjust as it may be, it would hardly matter if she could not hear dragons.

He promised Laconia he would have a dragon-hearing mistress, and he would keep that promise. Or there would be no mistress of his home at all.

Epilogue

Late September 1809

ANNE SAT IN an afternoon sunbeam on a little white bench in her mother's garden among the colorful autumn asters, gladioli, and delphiniums, and straightened the shawl over her shoulders. The bee balm had faded, though the humming bees kept busy in the fragrant new blossoms. The worn wooden bench with its odd rough patches and less than perfect symmetry was a new addition, moved here from another part of the garden so she could read and occasionally write in the midst of the garden dragons. Mother's commonplace book suggested that had been her practice as well. It seemed a good thing to be accessible to them—and to be away from Father's and Elizabeth's changeable tempers. They did not appreciate being thwarted in their plans.

To say Father was angry to learn of Mr. Elliot's matrimonial plans would be—well a dragon-sized understatement. After trying to bully Mr. Elliot into obedience and failing, he threw Mr. Elliot out without regard to the lateness of the hour or the angry weather threatening. Elizabeth was hardly more gracious, waxing on and on about how she had been used so ill by the ungrateful villain. Convenient, so very convenient.

But all was not glum. Beebalm seemed to like her company, particularly after Anne's intervention that removed Jet's threat. Come to think of it, the fairy dragons had become far more personable after that as well.

Summer tried to cling to its rights to the estate, but the first signs of autumn tinged every breeze. She would soon have to trade her shawl for a warmer spencer, or even a pelisse. What did dragons do in the winter? She would have to ask.

"I heard that the post came." Lady Russell loudly announced her arrival from across the flower bed. She no longer bothered with the garden paths when only Anne was around. Her long legs enabled her to step over and around the plants without disturbing them, blue head feathers bobbing over her eyes.

Odd, now that she had become accustomed to Lady Russell's dragon-form, it no longer startled her. In fact, it was difficult to recall what her woman-form had looked like.

Her personality, though, had not changed a mite. Seen through a draconic lens, her forceful controlling nature looked a bit more like boldness, making it a bit easier to tolerate.

"I suppose that is your way of inquiring if a letter from the Order has arrived."

Lady Russell paused and blinked her huge glittering eyes several times. "You have been worrying about it quite a bit."

It seemed that she was finally growing more accustomed to Anne returning boldness for boldness. Not that she always appreciated it, but she did tolerate it—not that she had any real choice. Father and Elizabeth were not so amenable. There, Anne had to tread more lightly.

She held up a missive sealed with blue wax. "I thought you would want to be with me as I read it."

"You could have let me know."

"And deny the fairy dragons their chief occupation? Perish the thought." Said fairy dragons, Peony, Wren-catcher, Aster and a particularly cheeky one that called herself Ladybird, twittered and circled overhead. Eager little gossips.

"You will spoil them, then where will we all be?" Lady Russell fanned her wings and scolded until the harem darted off into the trees, just close enough that they might still overhear something interesting.

Anne cracked the seal and unfolded the letter.

"So then, what do they say?" Lady Russell came along behind her and peered at the paper over her shoulder. "Do go on, tell me."

Was she humoring her, or could she not read? Anne was beginning to suspect the latter, but it would be rude to directly address it. All boldness aside, the Elliots were not the only beings with pride, and it would not do to wound it carelessly.

Anne traced the cross-written lines with her fingertip. "They say—oh that is interesting. They say that they are disappointed in Mr. Elliot's decision to disregard the recommendations of the Order with regard to his upcoming marriage."

"Well, they should be. A great deal more than simply disappointed, I should say. Horrid, disagreeable creature!"

"But they do not hold me accountable for his decision." Anne sighed and looked skyward. They did not blame her for him. Weights fell off her shoulders, and she breathed unencumbered for the first time since he had left. "They acknowledge the limitations of my situation and offer their continued support for my position as junior Keeper."

"Well, they certainly should. You are doing a very good job, indeed." Lady Russell glanced toward the trees as if intending the fairy dragons to hear what she had said.

"The census report we sent of the local wild dragons was well received, although not perfect. They have included a list of details, particularly: the nature of the relations between the wild dragons; when they arrived; and what drain they place on the territory, that should be included in the next report we send them."

"Naturally. Why would I have expected them to be satisfied with anything?" Lady Russell snorted and stomped. She never took suggestions of imperfection well.

"It seems Shelby is pleased with the recent turn of events. He has communicated that to the Order, which has been put to my credit. He is such a dear soul."

"The soul of a sheep dog, I am certain. I have never known a less drake-like and more dog-like creature in all my life."

"It seems he is not draconic enough for you. I think you would like him better if he breathed fire and growled whilst herding the sheep. Better still, he should sprout wings and fly over them, scolding the entire time."

Lady Russell chittered and clapped her beak, almost nipping Anne's ear. She might never grow accustomed to being teased—it was a rather new sensation for Anne to tease, but a pleasant one that would likely make Lady Russell's acerbic tendencies far more tolerable.

"Oh, that is unusual. I did not anticipate that." Anne squinted and turned the letter to continue reading the crossways lines. "They say that Mr. Elliot inquired about the estate charter, but since he was not yet the owner of the estate—and I infer that he is also not in their good graces at the moment—they refused to provide it to him. He was not pleased and, in their words, 'stormed out muttering invectives and epithets unbecoming of a Dragon Mate.' Heavens, that does not sound good."

"Nasty warm-blood. He wanted to see the charter? Whatever for?"

"He did not offer a specific reason to me when I asked, but did seem rather put out that I did not know anything about it. After Mr. Elliot left, I did ask Father if he knew where the document might be. He says it is somewhere in the house, but naturally, he is not certain where. I am, though, welcome to look for it so long as I do not cause any disruptions in doing so."

"How generous of him."

"Would I be disagreeable to remark how inconvenient it is that Elizabeth must be kept ignorant of all things draconic? It is quite vexing."

"It does not help that she is rather vexing even

without that." Lady Russell snorted.

She was right. "Mr. Wynn goes on to say that I should continue in my efforts to improve the affairs of the dragon estate—have we yet determined when Kellynch is likely to awaken?—and they will work towards some solution with Mr. Elliot for when that time comes." Anne set the letter aside and stared into the sky. "I suppose it is ungrateful of me to say I do not like the uncertainty of it all. I would very much like to have an answer now—to any of it: when Kellynch might awaken; how he will respond to the changes in the estate; if those efforts will be enough; what will be done with Mr. Elliot; if I will even remain Keeper here."

"I do not like it, either. Not at all." She laid her chin on Anne's shoulder. Warm and affectionate and motherly. "But I have been giving it no little thought. I have no answers for what will come with Mr. Elliot or any of the decisions the Blue Order might make. I do, though, have an idea—an alternative that might be useful if things take a certain turn—that I think you might find agreeable."

Anne craned her neck to peer into Lady Russell's wide, sparkling eyes. "I seem to recall you suggested that I marry Mr. Elliot."

"I know, but that was before his true nature was revealed. Have I argued with your reasons for refusing him?"

No, she had not, but it was difficult to tell if it was for Anne's sake or for her own. After all, a man with Mr. Elliot's attitudes would hardly be favorably disposed to a creature like Lady Russell.

Wentworth would have been different, though. Certainly, he would have. Did Lady Russell persuade her against him because he did not hear dragons, or because he did? Had she feared she could not persuade him of her identity as the widow Lady Russell or was it something more, like the way she feared Mr. Elliot would find a way to use her for his own gain? Wentworth would have never done such a thing—Anne knew his character well enough to be certain of that. But it was all really a moot point. Lady Russell would not own to anything she might have done, and they would likely never see Wentworth again.

Lady Russell stood straight and stepped over the bench to face Anne. "You know that if Mr. Elliot does inherit the estate, I will not be able to stay at Kellynch. I will have to find another place to live."

"Will that be a problem? Is that something that we should be seeking even now?" For all Lady Russell's foibles and peculiarities, it would be difficult to lose her oldest friend.

"I have been looking into the matter. I do have friends, you know."

"You have never introduced me. Who are they?"

"No one of consequence to you. The material issue, though, is that I do believe I will be able to secure a cottage in the country that will be quite adequate. It is not unusual for a … a woman, a widow … like myself to have a companion with her. I thought perchance, if you are agreeable … well, I should very much like your company. We have been friends for so very long now, that it would seem quite odd to be without you. You might come with me and live as companion to this widow in a small neighborhood, in a quiet situation. Sir Henry left me sufficient means. I think it could be quite comfortable."

"So then, what you are saying is that if I do not retain the Keepership at Kellynch, you would like me to Keep your new establishment? Or are you offering to Keep me?"

Lady Russell turned her head this way and that, finally hunching into her thinking posture. "A dragon keeping a person? What a very odd thought. You are becoming quite a peculiar girl since visiting that Blue Order of yours."

"Perhaps I am, my friend, perhaps I am." And, though neither her father, nor her sisters, nor possibly even Lady Russell might approve, it was not a bad thing at all.

Enjoy other books in the Series:

Pemberley: Mr. Darcy's Dragon
Longbourn: Dragon Entail
Netherfield: Rogue Dragon
A Proper Introduction to Dragons
The Dragons of Kellynch
Kellynch: Dragon Persuasion

For more dragon lore check out:
Elizabeth's Commonplace Book of Dragons
and
Dragon Myths of England
At RandomBitofFascination.com

Acknowledgments

So many people have helped me along the journey taking this from an idea to a reality.
Debbie, Diana, Anji, Susanne, Jan and Ruth thank you so much for cold reading and being honest! Your help is worth your weight in gold!
My dear friend Cathy, my biggest cheerleader, you have kept me from chickening out more than once!
And my sweet sister Gerri who believed in even those first attempts that now live in the file drawer!
Thank you!

❧Other Books by Maria Grace

Jane Austen's Dragons Series:
Pemberley: Mr. Darcy's Dragon
Longbourn: Dragon Entail
Netherfield:Rogue Dragon
A Proper Introduction to Dragons
The Dragons of Kellynch
Kellynch: Dragon Persuasion

Remember the Past
The Darcy Brothers
Fine Eyes and Pert Opinions

A Jane Austen Regency Life Series:
A Jane Austen Christmas: Regency Christmas Traditions
Courtship and Marriage in Jane Austen's World
How Jane Austen Kept her Cool: An A to Z History of Georgian Ice Cream

The Queen of Rosings Park Series:
Mistaking Her Character
The Trouble to Check Her
A Less Agreeable Man

Sweet Tea Stories:
A Spot of Sweet Tea: Hopes and Beginnings
Snowbound at Hartfield
A Most Affecionate Mother
Inspriation

Darcy Family Christmas Series:
Darcy and Elizabeth: Christmas 1811

The Darcy's First Christmas
From Admiration to Love

Given Good Principles Series:
Darcy's Decision
The Future Mrs. Darcy
All the Appearance of Goodness
Twelfth Night at Longbourn

Behind the Scene Anthologies (with Austen Variations):
Pride and Prejudice: Behind the Scenes
Persuasion: Behind the Scenes

Non-fiction Anthologies
Castles, Customs, and Kings Vol. 1
Castles, Customs, and Kings Vol. 2
Putting the Science in Fiction

Available in e-book, audiobook and paperback

Available in paperback, e-book, and audiobook format at all online bookstores.

On Line Exclusives at:

www.http//RandomBitsofFascination.com

Bonus and deleted scenes
Regency Life Series

Free e-books:
Rising Waters: Hurricane Harvey Memoirs
Lady Catherine's Cat
A Gift from Rosings Park
Bits of Bobbin Lace
Half Agony, Half Hope: New Reflections on Persuasion
Four Days in April

About the Author

Six-time BRAG Medallion Honoree, #1 Best-selling Historical Fantasy author Maria Grace has her PhD in Educational Psychology and is a 16-year veteran of the university classroom where she taught courses in human growth and development, learning, test development and counseling. None of which have anything to do with her undergraduate studies in economics/sociology/managerial studies/behavior sciences. She pretends to be a mild-mannered writer/cat-lady, but most of her vacations require helmets and waivers or historical costumes, usually not at the same time.

She writes Gaslamp fantasy, historical romance and non-fiction to help justify her research addiction.

She can be contacted at:

author.MariaGrace@gmail.com

Facebook:
http://facebook.com/AuthorMariaGrace

On Amazon.com:
http://amazon.com/author/mariagrace

Random Bits of Fascination
(http://RandomBitsofFascination.com)

Austen Variations (http://AustenVariations.com)

English Historical Fiction Authors
(http://EnglshHistoryAuthors.blogspot.com)

White Soup Press (http://whitesouppress.com/)

On Twitter @WriteMariaGrace

On Pinterest: http://pinterest.com/mariagrace423/

Made in the USA
Middletown, DE
21 August 2021